"I Couldn't Go Off And Leave You."

He glanced around the clearing and stood up. "Especially since you don't know a word of Spanish. Besides, the evil Victor has a weakness for blondes. If he'd gotten wind of your visit he would have torn up the village to find you. And Victor isn't very kind to his lady friends."

Melanie shivered. She was glad Justin had decided to take her with him. Grasping the hand he offered her, she pulled herself up to stand beside him. "I've always wanted some adventure in my life. Now's my chance!" She grinned up at him with such a look of excitement and expectation that he almost groaned.

She had no idea what might be in store for them, and he didn't have the heart to explain. Maybe she would never need to know men like Victor Degas.

Justin would do everything in his power to protect her from them.

Dear Reader,

Welcome to Silhouette! Our goal is to give you hours of unbeatable reading pleasure, and we hope you'll enjoy each month's six new Silhouette Desires. These sensual, provocative love stories are both believable and compelling—sometimes they're poignant, sometimes humorous, but always enjoyable.

Indulge yourself. Experience all the passion and excitement of falling in love along with our heroine as she meets the irresistible man of her dreams and together they overcome all obstacles in the path to a happy ending.

If this is your first Desire, I hope it'll be the first of many. If you're already a Silhouette Desire reader, thanks for your support! Look for some of your favorite authors in the coming months: Stephanie James, Diana Palmer, Dixie Browning, Ann Major and Doreen Owens Malek, to name just a few.

Happy reading!

Isabel Swift
Senior Editor

SDRL-7/85

ANNETTE BROADRICK
Heat of the Night

Silhouette Desire

Published by Silhouette Books New York

America's Publisher of Contemporary Romance

SILHOUETTE BOOKS
300 East 42nd St., New York, N.Y. 10017

ISBN: 0-373-05314-2

First Silhouette Books printing November 1986

America's Publisher of Contemporary Romance

Printed in the U.S.A.

Books by Annette Broadrick

Silhouette Romance

Circumstantial Evidence #329
Provocative Peril #359
Sound of Summer #412
Unheavenly Angel #442

Silhouette Desire

Hunter's Prey #185
Bachelor Father #219
Hawk's Flight #242
Deceptions #272
Choices #283
Heat of the Night #314

ANNETTE BROADRICK

lives on the shores of The Lake of the Ozarks in Missouri where she spends her time doing what she loves most—reading and writing romantic fiction. "For twenty-five years I lived in various large cities, working as a legal secretary, a very high-stress occupation. I never thought I was capable of making a career change at this point in my life, but thanks to Silhouette I am now able to write full time in the peaceful surroundings that have turned my life into a dream come true."

To Bev Saulsbury. . .
living proof that a next-door neighbor
can become a best friend

One

The cold rain beat down relentlessly upon every surface around her. Melanie Montgomery shivered once again as she used her coat as an umbrella, holding it over her head until her arms ached, feeling the weight of the water as it ran down the length of the lightweight material and dripped monotonously onto the river of mud surrounding her. Her shoes had long since disappeared beneath the swamplike surface of the road on which she stood.

Peering out at the dismal surroundings from under the collar of her coat hanging limply over her eyes, Melanie gazed at the fog hovering over much of the terrain below her, mercifully masking the Colombian jungle. Jagged mountain peaks towered along the horizon, needlessly reminding her that she was a long way from home.

For the first time since she had received Maria Teresa's invitation to visit, Melanie questioned the wisdom of her hasty decision.

Her mother had certainly recited all the many reasons she would be foolish to go, listing by chapter and verse all the horrible things that could happen to a young women traveling alone in a foreign country.

Melanie had been listening to her mother's dire warnings for years. Being the youngest in the family could be a real pain at times. Her brother Paul and her sister Elise were several years older than she, and for some reason none of them could seem to recognize that at twenty-five, Melanie no longer needed their loving protection. She was an adult. However, from the way her family carried on at times, they obviously thought of her as a rebellious adolescent.

Philip had offered the dubious escape of marriage, but that solution was too drastic just to get away from her family's overprotectiveness. She loved them all, but had decided enough is enough. Even long distance Elise had the irritating habit of hovering despite the fact she had two energetic children to take up her time at home.

So Melanie had ignored all of her mother's gruesome predictions of catastrophe and had single-mindedly prepared for her trip to South America.

It was that same single-mindedness that had caused her small gift shop to grow and prosper in the three years since she had finished college. She was proud of her success. People drove from miles around the small town nestled in the rolling hills of northeastern Tennessee to see what new ideas and unique gifts she had to offer.

Maria Teresa's invitation had come at a time when Melanie had recognized that much of the challenge from her business was gone and she was bored. A trip south might give her new ideas as well as help her to find exotic gifts that would sell back in the States.

She and Maria Teresa had been roommates at college for four years, and every time Maria Teresa returned to her home near Villa Vicencias, Colombia, she had begged Melanie to come with her, but something had always intervened. This time Melanie was determined to take her friend up on her offer.

Now all Melanie had to do was to find a way to get there.

She glanced around the dripping countryside and sighed. Oh, to have a mass-transit bus suddenly appear out of the fog and whisk her the rest of the way. From what she could see of the dismal surroundings, she could very well be the only soul on the planet— except for her guide, Julio.

She peered through the murky haze trying to get a glimpse of him. All she could see was his automobile several hundred feet down the mountainside, half buried beneath the sea of mud that had cascaded down the mountainside earlier.

Without Julio's quick thinking both of them would have gone over the side of the mountain together with the car. When he saw that the giant mud slide was going to catch them in its flow he had yelled at her to jump, which she had done with surprising strength, landing full length in the slime of the Colombian mountain mud.

After the car had stopped sliding down the mountainside, Julio carefully followed the steeply sloped path to see if there was a possibility of rescuing his livelihood. Melanie watched as he made his way around the car, shaking his head dismally. Even from her position on the road, Melanie could see there was little hope of moving the car short of employing a crane of some sort.

Glancing around the primitive countryside, she seriously doubted that one would suddenly materialize.

According to the map, Villa Vicencias was approximately eighty miles from Bogotá. In Tennessee, eighty miles could be driven in less than two hours. Unfortunately, the same couldn't be said for Colombia. A mountain range ran between the two cities and the elevation rose from eighty-six hundred feet above sea level in Bogotá to over twelve thousand feet in the mountains. Then the road dropped into the surrounding jungle to Villa Vicencias, which was approximately six hundred feet above sea level. As best as she could determine, Melanie was somewhere in the mountains with no transportation and no signs of civilization in any direction.

I wonder what Elise would do in this situation? she thought a little wistfully. But then Elise would never find herself in such a situation. Elise had never made an impulsive decision in her life.

One of her mother's most irritating habits was comparing Melanie to Elise when she wanted to make a point. Elise had never had the itch to travel. She had gone to college, become a nurse and settled down to a predictable life. After an unfortunate marriage Elise had met and married Damon Trent and was now ecstatically happy playing mother to their two children.

Melanie could almost hear her mother's voice saying, "Why can't you be more like your sister?" Her jaw tightened at the thought. She and Elise were poles apart in personality, although they shared similar looks. Both were blond, but Melanie's coloring emphasized their Scandinavian blood. Her blond hair was almost silver, very thick yet fine and she was glad at the moment that she had taken the time to braid it before leaving Bogotá. The one long braid had come unwound from the nape of her neck, and mud indiscriminately covered it, as well as the rest of her.

Her eyes were the same shade of green as Elise's and they were both tall, but that was where the resemblance ended. Melanie rushed out and embraced life with open arms. As a child, her inquisitive nature and need to understand everything around her had driven others to distraction trying to answer her questions.

Straightening her shoulders, Melanie reminded herself that she had gotten herself into the present situation, so she had better figure a way out of it. She wasn't in the States now, where she could hike to the nearest home and ask to use the telephone. She hadn't seen anyone else on the road in the past several hours, and there was no sign of life anywhere. A sudden shiver coursed through her. Never had she felt so helpless and alone.

"Julio? Where are you?" She peered through the rain, feeling more miserable by the minute.

She heard a scrambling noise nearby and whirled around. Her guide pulled himself to his feet, ineffectively wiping the mud and water from his face.

"I'm very sorry, Señorita Montgomery, but I cannot get your luggage from the automobile."

Melanie gave silent thanks to her presence of mind when she grabbed her purse as she jumped from the car, although it wasn't too surprising. She had kept a death grip on it ever since she landed in the country, for fear it would be stolen. At least she had her passport and money, but where was she going to find a place to use it?

"What are we going to do?" she asked.

Julio shrugged. Julio, who Melanie guessed to be in his late forties, had been both helpful and friendly during the trip from Bogotá. He had loquaciously described his family to her. He had six children, two of whom were grown and living in Cartagena, and had further expounded on how fortunate he was to have such a marvelous piece of machinery that enabled him to make a satisfactory living for them all.

They both gazed down the mountainside with despair. Melanie was stranded. Julio's livelihood had just slithered down the muddy side of the mountain. Gloom settled over them as they took stock of their situation.

Finally Julio spoke. "There is a small village ahead, but I'm afraid it is several miles away. There is no help for it. We will have to walk."

Melanie wondered if she looked as bedraggled as he did and had a hunch that she looked even worse, if possible. At least she had her coat as some protection from the elements. Julio stood before her in khakis and a light-weight jacket, their color hidden under the mud that covered him. She was glad she had no way of knowing what she looked like at the moment.

Nodding with a show of courage that was somewhat lacking, Melanie turned in the direction that Julio had pointed and began to walk, the mud sucking at her shoes with every step.

Justin Drake sat at a large conference table with four other men in an office building in Buenos Aires and concentrated on Jorge Villaneuva's words. Although he had spent a large portion of the past twelve months in Argentina, and fluently spoke the language, Justin needed all of his linguistic skills in order to follow the rapid-fire speech of the man with whom he was dealing.

He leaned forward in his chair, the smooth cut of his custom-made cream jacket pulling tightly across his wide shoulders. His tawny-colored hair emphasized the burnished tan of his face and neck, and his expression denoted his intense concentration, the slight frown above his nose a clear warning to his companions that nothing would be overlooked during the negotiations. His steel-blue eyes gave none of his thoughts away.

"You must understand," Jorge said in Spanish, "that it is also to my company's advantage to approve a joint venture with Trent Enterprises, your company, but I cannot make the decision without the consent of my directors. Surely you can see that."

Justin allowed himself a slight smile. The man was definitely nervous, which was exactly what Justin had intended. Justin had represented Trent Enterprises in South America for several years now, and he recognized the clout he carried because of the name. Damon would be pleased with the present negotiations.

"Of course I understand," Justin responded, also in Spanish. "However, we need an answer within forty-eight hours, otherwise I will need to make other arrangements."

"But that is impossible!" Jorge exploded into speech. "I cannot possibly contact everyone and set up a special meeting in that length of time—you must see that I cannot do this...." He paused because the door opened after a perfunctory tap.

Justin glanced up and saw his secretary peeking around the door uncertainly. "Yes, Maria?"

"Excuse me, Señor Drake. Señor Trent is calling from Chicago. He said he must speak with you immediately."

Justin glanced at Jorge and noticed the man had lost some of his color. Even the name of Damon Trent could create a certain tension in those people who hoped that by working through Justin they could somehow win an advantage.

Justin stood, nodding to Maria. "If you'll excuse me for a moment, Jorge. I'll take the call in my office."

He strode from the room. Entering his office, he sat down behind the desk and picked up the phone.

"Damon?"

"I can barely hear you," came the weak reply. "Can you hear me?"

"Fairly well, Damon. Did Maria tell you I was in conference with Jorge Villaneuva?"

"Yes. Sorry to interrupt but this can't wait."

The line cleared up and Damon's voice rang over the phone, the note of urgency unmistakable.

"What's wrong?"

"How soon could you leave Buenos Aires?"

"What do you mean, leave? I'm right in the middle of some very delicate negotiations."

"I know that, and I wouldn't ask if this weren't an emergency. I need your help."

Damon Trent was more than Justin's employer. He was closer to him than any other human being. Damon rarely asked for help from anyone, and Justin tensed. Something was drastically wrong. "You've got it, Damon. Tell me what to do."

"I need you to go to Bogotá as soon as possible. Elise's sister has disappeared."

Justin felt a strong surge of coldness sweep over him. "Melanie has disappeared in Colombia? What the hell is she doing down here?"

"Elise said she was planning to visit a college chum. She flew down there three days ago and promised to let us know when she arrived. We haven't heard a word. When we checked with her friend, she hadn't heard anything from her, either. She thought Melanie had been delayed leaving home."

"Do you know if she ever arrived in Colombia?"

"Yes. She spent the first night at the Tequendama in Bogotá but checked out early the next morning. We don't know where she went from there but assume she rented a car to drive her to Villa Vicencias, where her friend lives."

"Dammit, she has no business traveling on her own, Damon!"

"Try telling her that," Damon replied dryly.

"Don't worry. She'll hear plenty from me when I find her."

"Then you think she's all right?"

Justin could hear the worry in Damon's voice. For a moment Justin allowed himself to picture all that could have happened to a young woman alone in Colombia and felt himself growing even colder.

"I'll find her, Damon," he said carefully side-stepping the question. "I'm on my way."

"Thanks, Justin. Elise and I really appreciate your help."

"I'm just glad you let me know. I wish you had told me about her plans sooner."

"Quite frankly, we didn't know about them. By the time her mother called to tell us, Melanie had already left Tennessee."

Justin had only met Melanie once and that had been a few years back. She had been a schoolgirl then, with sparkling green eyes and a flashing smile. He had stopped by Damon's home in Chicago and found Elise's sister visiting them for the week. Although young, she had appeared to know what she wanted to do with her life. He had noticed that she became defensive with Elise whenever her sister questioned her plans for the future. At the time he had thought that she was a potential rebel. Her latest escapade tended to confirm his opinion.

Justin shook his head. He didn't have time to go chasing around the countryside looking for a foolish little rebel out to prove something to her family. On the other hand, she could be in serious trouble. He thought too much of Damon and Elise not to do everything in his power to help ease their concern about her.

Realizing that Damon was still waiting patiently on the other end of the line, Justin concluded, "I'll be in touch."

"Fine. Oh, and Justin—"

"Yes?"

"Don't take any chances. Find out what's happened, but don't try to be a hero or anything."

"Who, me? I've spent too many years in boardrooms and behind desks. I'm not in any condition to be playing hero."

"Just so you remember that. I happen to recall how you spent the few years prior to your employment with me."

"Oh, that."

"Yes."

"Glad you reminded me. I may have to call on some of my old contacts."

He heard a sigh. "I sincerely hope not."

"I'll get back to you."

"Thanks, Justin."

"Don't mention it."

Justin hung up the phone and stared at it for a few moments, thinking furiously. Then he picked it up again and buzzed Maria. "Book me on the next flight to Bogotá," he said when she answered. "Leave the return flight open."

Once again he lowered the phone. He would need to go to his apartment and pack. His business suit would have no place in some of the areas he remembered in Colombia. Of all the countries Melanie could have chosen to disappear in, Colombia was the worst one for him to be forced to enter. After the close call he had a few years ago, he had vowed never to return. The trouble with making sweeping statements was they had a tendency to come back to haunt a person. He started toward the door when he remembered Jorge Villaneuva.

Opening the door to the conference room, he went back to the meeting. The four men looked up, hoping to read something from his expression, but they were disappointed.

"I'm sorry to break up this meeting, gentlemen," he said in smooth Spanish, the switch in languages coming easily and naturally to him, "but I'm afraid I must. I'm needed elsewhere."

The reaction to his announcement couldn't have been better from his point of view as a businessman. They were now convinced he didn't care whether or not they shared in the new venture with Trent Enterprises or not. Otherwise, how could he cavalierly plan to walk out of the delicate negotiations presently pending?

He opened the door for them, and they filed past him. "I will be in touch, hopefully in the next week or so."

"Week or so!" Jorge repeated in shocked tone. "Then Mr. Trent has decided against us?"

"I didn't say that."

"Ah, but you've made the urgency clear. Please, give me a few hours and I will get back with you."

"I don't have the few hours at the moment. I have a plane to catch."

"Where can I find you? I will call as soon as I get the approval necessary."

Justin thought for a moment. He would probably stay at the same hotel where Melanie had gone. "You can leave word for me at the Tequendama in Bogotá."

"You're going to Colombia?"

"Yes." Damon could see the wheels turning in Jorge's head. If he were trying to place some business connotation on the sudden trip, he was going to have a hell of a time. Trent Enterprises had no business connections in Colombia.

"I will contact you as soon as possible," Jorge assured him, and quickly left.

Justin's mind had already returned to the problem at hand. What could have happened to Melanie?

Several hours later he was still asking himself the same question.

Her fair coloring had made her easily memorable, and Justin had no trouble finding people in Bogotá who confirmed that she had in fact stayed at the hotel. However, no one seemed to know where she was going when she left.

The desk clerk remembered her checking out and vaguely recalled someone helping her with her luggage as she left, but rental cars were easily come by in the city and he could not remember who she had contacted.

Eventually Justin gave up in frustration. He would have to rent a car himself and follow the same route that she would have had to take in order to get across the mountain range to the interior.

The constant rain didn't help matters. After he found a car and driver, he was quickly informed that the roads between the two towns were not the best and with the heavy rains there were bound to be washouts and slides. Justin hoped that the weather was all that had delayed her. He would love to see that lady soon. There were a few pertinent facts of life he intended to teach her about traveling alone in a foreign country. He only hoped she hadn't already been forced to learn some of them.

* * *

Never in her life had Melanie been so miserable. It had been after dark by the time she and Julio had finally stumbled into the town. It was a small settlement, and because of the inclement weather, the streets were deserted. She was glad that Julio was in charge. He managed to find rooms for them to stay and began to make arrangements to try to salvage his car. There was still a chance her luggage could be rescued.

Never had she felt so alone. Her sparse knowledge of Spanish was worthless; these people talked too rapidly for her to catch more than a word or two. There were no phones in the village and no way for her to contact Maria Teresa. She wondered what she should do—try to get back to Bogotá or find another car to continue into the interior.

The next morning she no longer cared what happened. She was feverish and miserable, her hours of exposure causing her chilled body to rebel. Everything became hazy, and people faded in and out of her vision. During the next several hours she was certain her mother was there fussing about her, fluffing her pillows and straightening her covers, all the while pointing out the foolishness of her trip. At other times Elise seemed to appear with her gentle tones and soothing hands to sponge away the heat of her body and see that she ate something. She tried to make them understand how important it was for her to be independent of them. The emotional ties seemed to be strangling her.

They didn't seem to understand. Instead they murmured soft sounds of comfort and continued to care for her.

"The mud slides have closed the roads," Justin's driver unnecessarily pointed out, pulling up by the side of the road.

Although it was not raining at the moment the clouds hung low and threatening, and Justin's inner alarm was working overtime. Had Melanie been caught in that sudden deluge of mud and debris? He crawled out of the car and walked to the edge of the road. The precipitous drop did nothing to reassure him.

"What do you wish to do, *señor*? I cannot go any further."

Good question. There was only one answer. "I'll have to go by foot. Here." He handed the man some money.

The driver looked at him as though he had lost his mind. "You mean you intend to stay here?"

"No. I intend to continue looking for my friend."

"But, *señor*, how will you get back to Bogotá?"

"I'll worry about that later."

The driver shrugged, convinced that all *norteamericanos* were loco.

Justin had prepared himself for a trek, if necessary. His clothes were rugged, his boots were made for rough terrain, his jacket waterproof, and he had packed what he thought he might need in a backpack. He removed his belongings from the car and hefted the pack over his shoulders, taking care to settle the straps comfortably. From the looks of things he had a long hike ahead of him.

He saw the car an hour later and spent another hour working his way down the mountainside to see if anyone was in it. If they were, he didn't give them much hope for surviving. Peering into the windows, he was relieved to find it empty, but he saw a scarf laying in the front seat that he knew belonged to Melanie. He remembered Elise remarking on its unusual design when she bought it for her.

Justin wasn't sure what he felt. On the one hand, he was relieved to know he was on the right track. On the other, he couldn't help but wonder if she'd been hurt and where she was at that moment. He peered around him and saw nothing but jungle foliage down below and rugged mountain peaks above. Not the hospitable climate either of them was used to, although he knew he was better prepared than Melanie to survive in such surroundings.

Justin had learned more than he ever cared to know about Colombia when he had worked in the narcotics division of a federal task force several years ago. It was ironic that after vowing never to return to the country he should be here on a rescue mission. If certain parties recognized him he would be the one in need of rescuing. But he'd had no choice in the matter. Damon was right. He was the only one who would know where to look and how to find her.

The long hike to the small village could have been worse—at least the rain had held off until he arrived, but then it came down in torrents. Justin watched the heavy rainfall from the slight protection of a metal overhang from the local hotel, if the small adobe building could be considered as such. The room he had rented barely held the small single bed, and indoor bathrooms had not been considered essential when the building was designed.

At least it was dry. As tired as he was, he would have no trouble sleeping.

He had asked about Melanie and was told that a woman fitting her description had come into the village a day or so before but, because she was alone except for her guide, had found a room in a private home. After one of the men had told him where to find her, Justin stood there wondering if he should wait until morning rather than to brave the elements once more just to let her know what he thought about her harebrained vacation plans. The man who had brought her to the village had seemed relieved to turn over the responsibility of her safety to someone else and had offered to try to retrieve her belongings as soon as possible.

Justin had been a little surprised at the surge of physical weakness that had enveloped him when he finally caught up with her and learned that she was all right. Now that his imaginings had been proven false, he could feel the anger building within him. He knew he needed time to gain control over his emotions. From everything he knew about Melanie, she wasn't going to be all that pleased that he had come after her. Not that it mattered. The sooner he could get her out of Colombia and back home, the better, regardless of how she felt about it.

He shrugged. It was too early for her to be in bed. He might as well inform her of his presence in the village. He lifted his hood over his head and dashed across the square and down the village road where he had been told she was staying. He met no one on the way, and found the small cottage with no trouble.

The trouble came when the door swung open and a middle-aged woman greeted his explanations with voluble relief. "I am so glad you have come for the pretty blond lady. Thank God you have come. She is sick, and I've been unable to keep her fever down. Maybe you can help. Come with me, please."

Justin's heart sank. Surely Melanie had had all of her vaccinations. He followed the woman into the room and down a short hallway. She opened the door and stepped back, obviously waiting for him to go inside.

The voluble woman ushered him into a small bedroom, where a kerosene lamp burned on a small table by the bed. The woman lying there bore little resemblance to the schoolgirl he remembered. Melanie—the young girl—had been striking. Melanie—the woman—was breathtakingly beautiful.

Her wide-set eyes were closed, their thick lashes resting against flushed cheeks. Justin felt the urge to stroke her satiny cheek to see if it was as smooth as it appeared to be.

The sight of her lying there so still in those primitive surroundings caused a gutwrenching reaction within him. She looked so vulnerable—so alone.

What had caused her to take such a gamble with her safety? This was no impulsive schoolgirl. Whatever her family might think, she was a woman, the soft flowing lines beneath the light covers testified to that. Justin absently noted his body's reaction to her beauty.

He walked over to the bed and sat down on its edge. Slowly he stroked her hair from her forehead. Its long length had been carefully brushed and framed her face. He studied the delicate shape, the high cheekbones, the small straight nose and the shape of her delectable mouth. It looked as though it had been made to be kissed. He traced a line from her cheekbone to her chin, loving the feel of her skin but concerned about the fever. She was burning up.

Her eyelids slowly opened, and she stared up at him without surprise. "You might as well join the party," she whispered softly. "Everybody else in the family is here. Are you going to point out how foolish I've been, as well?"

Her reaction to his sudden presence was far from what he had expected. He glanced around the room. Her hostess had left them. Who did she think was there?

He picked up her small hand in his, feeling the heat, and slowly stroked her fingers with his other hand. "A party seems to be a good idea. What are we celebrating?'' he responded, trying to mask the worry in his voice.

"I've forgotten," she muttered. "It's so hot in here. Why doesn't someone turn on the air-conditioning?"

"They don't want you to catch cold." He smoothed his hand across her forehead once again.

She moved restlessly on the bed. "Elise should have warned me that you were coming."

He picked up the rag lying on the table and dipped it into a small bowl of water sitting there, then carefully cooled her face with it.

She wasn't making much sense.

"Elise didn't know where you were."

"Oh, she and Mom always know where I am. I swear they have some sort of tracking device that follows me around."

She sounded so disgusted Justin couldn't help but chuckle. A tracking device might have eased everyone's worrying.

"They love you."

She sighed, her eyes drifting closed once more. "I know. I love them, too, but I have to live my own life."

"Is that what you're doing in Colombia, living your own life?"

"I'm trying to, but the car went over the side of the mountain," she explained.

"I see. It's hard to be independent without a car."

She smiled—a soft, lazy smile that Justin found captivating. Her eyes opened, their green glitter reminding him of emeralds shooting sparks in sunlight.

"I know you're not real," she confided.

"I'm not?"

"Why would Justin Drake be here? And if he were, he certainly wouldn't have the patience to sit around and discuss my family problems with me."

"I would—I mean, he wouldn't? Why not?"

"Because Justin is one of those dynamic personalities that never stays in one place very long. He's too busy chasing all over the world conquering new frontiers."

Justin's brow rose slightly. "You don't sound impressed."

"Oh, he's all right, if you like that type. Personally, I've had my fill of dominating personalities." She seemed to be having trouble focusing her eyes. After blinking once or twice she apparently gave up and firmly closed them once more.

"You look so real," she complained.

He tried not to laugh and began to bathe her face once more.

"Why don't you go to sleep now," he said, brushing the wisps of hair away from her forehead.

She smiled. "What a silly suggestion. I'm already asleep."

He wasn't sure how to answer that. He leaned over to brush her cheek with his lips. She turned her head and his lips touched hers. Startled by the unexpected contact, Justin started to pull away, but the temptation was too great to ignore. He deepened the pressure on her mouth until her lips parted, their softness luring him to greater intimacy.

Melanie languidly slid her arms around his shoulders, her fingers burying themselves in the tawny thickness of his hair.

Her response electrified him, and his arms tightened around her. He moved his mouth slowly, expertly, over hers, learning its shape, exploring its depth, memorizing her.

Justin had a hunch that Melanie would be furious with him for taking advantage of her present state of mind. He decided it would be worth facing her anger at a later date to have her so responsive in his arms at the moment.

Two

___

Melanie slowly opened her eyes and blinked at the watery sunlight flooding the small room where she lay. Her head felt clear, and she had a distinct feeling of being hungry. She smiled and stretched. Whatever had ailed her seemed to have left sometime during the night and was probably searching right now for its next victim.

She wondered how long she had been ill. The days and nights had run together in a very muddled way. So had her dreams. Thinking of her dreams made her smile. All of her subconscious fears and desires had sprung full blown into glorious cinemalike tales. She had dreamed of being lost in the jungle, with rain beating down on her. She had dreamed of her mother—and later Elise and Damon—all lecturing her on the folly of her impulsiveness.

She had also dreamed of Justin Drake. For a person Melanie had only met once in her life, Justin Drake had certainly made an impression. She remembered everything about him—his height, his quiet strength, the way the sunlight glinted off his tawny hair, showing intermingled strands of gold and copper—the way the blue of his eyes shifted from a deep indigo to almost a silver, depending on his mood. He was quite a man.

Unfortunately he was the very type of man she had learned early in life to avoid. Unconsciously she recognized that a man such as Justin might jeopardize her basic need for freedom. Since their meeting years ago Melanie had carefully avoided seeing him again. In her opinion, what the eye doesn't see, the heart doesn't yearn for.

So it was strange that she should have dreamed about him. And what a dream. He had walked into the room as though he owned the place, as though he owned her, and she felt a slight tingle at the thought of belonging to him. Not that she had any intention of being any man's possession, but she had a hunch that Justin would definitely look after his own.

She had dreamed that Justin had sat down beside her, had held her hand, had kissed her. She had felt as though she were melting, her bones turning to liquid, when he had pulled her into his arms. His mouth had felt warm and firm, and very practiced. For a dream, the kiss had seemed very real, and she squirmed at the memory.

Melanie's stomach growled and she sat up, impatient with herself for wasting her time thinking about Justin Drake.

Pulling off the borrowed gown she wore, Melanie walked across the room to the pitcher of water waiting near a wash bowl and poured some of the liquid out, hastily bathing herself in the slight chill of the morning. She had to make plans today to try to find a way out of the village. She wondered if Julio had managed to rescue his car and her belongings.

The door opened behind her, and she turned to speak to her hostess. Instead of the friendly woman who had cared for her, Justin Drake stood in the doorway, looking from the bed to her in surprise.

He had expected to find her asleep. Instead she stood before him like a fragile nymph, her long hair falling around her, shielding her body from his eyes, her gaze wide and startled.

"What are *you* doing here?" she exclaimed in disbelief.

"What are you doing out of bed?" he asked at the same time.

Melanie fumbled for the gown she had discarded, feeling a flush cover her entire body.

"You have no business being out of bed," Justin said, stepping smoothly into the room and coming toward her.

Hastily folding the gown around her in a toga effect, she glared at him. "And you have no business walking into my room! Get out of here!"

He could see that she was shaking, and he wasn't sure whether it was due to weakness or anger. Perhaps it was a combination of the two. He set down the suitcase he had been holding and came closer to her. His voice softened as he placed his hand on her forearm and gently led her to the bed. "It's too soon for you to be out of bed. You're going to need a day or two to regain your strength."

Melanie had already discovered the truth of his words. She felt so weak her knees were threatening to buckle, but she wasn't at all sure her condition was due to her recent illness. It had more to do with this particular man showing up here so unexpectedly.

"What are you doing here?" she repeated weakly, sinking down onto the bed.

"I came to find you."

"Why?" she demanded.

"Your family was worried about you."

"I'm all right," she said defensively.

"Of course you are. Stranded in a native village and ill. You've probably never been better."

"They had no business sending you to look for me."

"Maybe not. But I'm here now, so you might as well let me help you."

"I don't need your help."

"Melanie, be reasonable. You don't even speak the language. Your guide has gone. What do you intend to do now?"

Julio was gone? She had counted on him to help her find transportation. Her Spanish had proven to be inadequate to make her needs known. She sighed with frustration.

"I intend to find my way out of here, walk if I have to, and get to Villa Vicencias."

He stared at her incredulously. "Do you mean you still intend to pay your friend a visit?"

"Certainly. Why shouldn't I?"

"Haven't you learned anything since you arrived? This is no place for a woman alone!"

"I refuse to comment on such a ridiculous statement."

"There's nothing ridiculous about it. You are no longer in the United States. Your attitude won't be tolerated down here."

"What attitude?"

"That you are capable of coping alone."

"But I am!"

"Melanie," he began, then stopped. Taking a deep breath, Justin paused and mentally counted to ten. "All right. So you can cope. However, now that I am here I would like to help you, if you will allow me to."

"How?"

"By getting you wherever you want to go."

"And how do you intend to do that?"

"First of all I need to find out where your friend lives, then I'll see about finding some transportation."

Melanie could feel the tight band of dread and fear leaving her for the first time since she and Julio had been nearly caught in the mud slide. Until now she hadn't even realized those emotions had existed within her. She also acknowledged to herself what a fraud she was.

Reaching out her hand, she touched Justin briefly as he leaned against the wall next to the bed. "I'm sorry for being rude. You're right. It will be much easier for me to have you make the arrangements."

He was surprised at her easy capitulation and wondered how recovered she actually was. Melanie Montgomery in true fighting form would never have been so acquiescent.

He straightened and gave her a smile that caused a queer jerking sensation in her chest. "I'll go see what I can find for you to eat." He gestured to the suitcase sitting by the door. "Julio managed to rescue your clothes. I thought that might help you to recover." He smiled once again, a slow smile that caused a shiver to run through her.

She hadn't dreamed Justin's presence, which meant the kiss they had exchanged had been very real. She flushed at the memory. How embarrassing. What must he think of her eagerness to fall into his arms? She stiffened at the thought.

I can't be held responsible for what I do or say when I'm sick. I'll just have to make it clear to him that my behavior was totally out of character. I'm not interested in him in any way!

With him out of the room Melanie eased herself off the bed once more and frantically searched for something to wear. At least Julio had stayed until he had delivered her clothes, for which she was thankful.

She found a pair of jeans and a long-sleeved sweater and quickly put them on, afraid any minute Justin would walk in again without a knock. Sliding her feet into her shoes, she crossed the room and hesitantly opened the door. The smell of food cooking lured her into the hallway and toward the kitchen.

"I thought I told you to stay in bed!" A voice spoke immediately behind her.

She jumped and whirled around, losing her balance. Justin caught her arms and steadied her, shaking his head. "You don't mind worth a damn, do you?"

"I'm not a child, Justin."

"I swear you act like one sometimes. You don't seem to have a grain of common sense about you."

"Thank you very much for that illuminating description of my intellect."

"You're welcome. It doesn't even cost extra."

They stood in the hallway, glaring at each other until Justin felt the slight trembling in her body. He eased his grip on her arms slightly and forced himself to relax. "You might as well go sit down at the table. Your breakfast is ready." He placed his hand in the small of her back and followed her into the kitchen.

Her hostess glanced around and greeted her with a wide smile and a volley of words. Unfortunately Melanie could only understand one or two of them. Something about her sickness as far as she could tell. Then she heard the word *esposo* and saw the woman glance at Justin with affectionate indulgence.

"Did you tell her you were my husband?" she asked incredulously.

"No, but I haven't denied it, either." He lifted one brow slightly. "What difference does it make what she thinks? We don't owe her any explanations."

She stared at him for a moment, thinking about the matter. Eventually she shrugged. "I guess you're right."

"My God, let's get this down in writing. You are actually going to concede that on one occasion I happened to be right. The heavens will probably open and a host of angels appear!"

"Sarcasm doesn't become you, Justin," Melanie managed to say primly, but her grin escaped despite all her efforts to remain solemn.

But that mischievous smile definitely becomes you, Justin thought as a tightness appeared in his chest. He wasn't sure how he was going to deal with his reaction to her, especially now that he knew how good she felt in his arms. He had agreed to look after her until he could get her to her destination. After that there would be no need for their paths to cross. She had already made her opinion of him clear. He didn't need a reminder.

Their hostess waved them to the table and Justin sat down beside Melanie on a rough-hewn bench, his arm brushing against hers while they ate. The food tasted delicious to Melanie, but she found she could eat very little. It was all she could do to sit there.

Justin glanced at her with a slight smile. "Care to admit I was right about it being too soon for you to be up, or are you going to pretend that you're ready to start hiking out of here?"

She shook her head slightly. "I don't understand why I feel so weak."

"Simple. You've had a debilitating fever and have been in bed for three days. Your body isn't ready to function on all cylinders just yet. But give it time. There's no rush to get out of here."

He was right, and there was no reason to try to prove that she was second cousin to Wonder Woman. With a certain amount of relief, Melanie returned to her room, stretched out on the bed and immediately fell into a deep, healing sleep.

By the time she woke up a couple of hours later, she was feeling much stronger. She went in search of her hostess and mimed that she wished to bathe and wash her hair.

The sun was out in full force by the time Melanie had bathed and dressed, so she decided to walk outside to enjoy the warmth and to dry her hair. She hadn't walked long until she found herself surrounded by a group of small chattering children, all pointing at her and giggling. She caught the phrase *ojos verde*, which she knew to mean green eyes. Her hair color was another point of interest.

Finding herself in a small square, she sat down on a bench and looked around. Her faithful followers gathered closer. She smiled at them, their large liquid brown eyes gazing at her, their brown little bodies in sharp contrast to her pale skin.

She tried talking with them and before long was giggling with them. They were so inquisitive—touching her skin, patting her hair and trying to investigate the contents of her purse. To discourage their prying, she pulled out her lipstick and a compact, letting each child look into the mirror. The giggles escalated to hilarity.

A little girl who appeared to be three years old or so climbed into her lap. Melanie showed her how the lipstick worked, carefully outlining the child's mouth. Eventually all the girls wanted some bright color on their lips, so Melanie patiently applied color to each one.

"You look like the Pied Piper."

Melanie glanced up to see Justin standing there, watching them. His hands rested on his hips and Melanie couldn't help but notice how the jeans he wore emphasized the long length of his legs. His soft chambray shirt clung to the wide expanse of his chest and shoulders, and her gaze wandered over his sleek, elegant body with unconscious admiration.

The memory of the kiss they had shared caused her to flush. She could still remember the silky feel of his hair between her fingers, still smell the musky scent of his after-shave, still taste the slight minty flavor of his mouth.

She forced herself to meet his gaze. "Have you had any luck finding us transportation?"

"Yes and no. There isn't anything here at the village, but I understand that if we follow the road south we should come across a large plantation. We should have a better chance of finding transportation there."

"When do you want to start?"

"When you're feeling stronger. I don't know how many miles we're talking about."

Melanie lifted the little girl out of her lap and stood up, dusting the back of her jeans. "I'm sure I'll feel up to it by morning. I already feel a hundred percent better than I did this morning."

He shrugged. "Whatever you say."

"I'm sure you're eager to get back to wherever you came from."

"Buenos Aires."

"Oh?" She smiled wistfully. "I've always wanted to go there."

He grinned. "You have a standing invitation to visit."

"Thank you."

He glanced up at the sun. "Are you about ready to eat? Rosa sent me to look for you."

"Is that her name? I never thought to ask." She turned around and waved at the children, throwing them kisses that caused a great deal of giggling. They started shouting and laughing, and she turned around to Justin. "What are they saying?"

"They don't want you to leave."

"Tell them I must go eat and that maybe I'll see them later."

Justin knelt down and began talking to the children. She watched as he spoke, his hands eloquent. He paused and laid his hand on the head of the closest boy. Smiling, he tousled his hair, then stood up and held out his hand to Melanie.

"Ready?"

She nodded, unable to express what the sight of him with the children had done to her.

They turned and started down the road. Justin glanced down at her as she kept pace with his long strides and grinned. "Rosa is quite taken with you, by the way. She told me I'm very lucky to have such a beautiful wife."

Melanie wasn't sure what to say.

"She also scolded me for allowing you to travel alone and wanted to know why I haven't moved in with you."

His dry comment caught Melanie off guard, and she could feel heat warm her cheeks. "I suppose you explained to her that we aren't married."

"No. I told her you needed your rest." He laughed at the expression on her face.

"Very funny," she muttered.

He ran his hand down the softly waving hair that fell over her shoulders and down to her waist. "I have never seen hair that color. It looks like spun silver."

She felt the warmth of his hand through her hair and clothes. It felt as though he had placed it on her bare skin. If they were going to be traveling together, she was going to have to learn to control her reaction to him. She just wished she didn't find him so darned attractive!

Justin noted her continued silence and mentally chastised himself. She didn't want to hear a bunch of compliments from him. Actually, she didn't want anything from him and would have been happier if he hadn't shown up at all.

He had a hunch that she would have managed just fine without him. Julio would not have left her until he could have found her some transportation, but since he had come this far, Justin decided to see that she made it safely to her friend's home.

He would never forget the picture she had made, sitting in that little square, surrounded by children. Her hair had glistened in the sunlight, and her smile warmed their hearts. No woman had ever affected him in quite the same way. She was unusually beautiful. He had known other women equally attractive, but she had a beauty of the spirit that drew him to her and caused him to want to protect her. Perhaps that same essence of vulnerability was what her family perceived. Yet it was their overprotectiveness that appeared to be driving her to act more and more independent.

We all need to learn to back off and let her try her wings, he reminded himself.

He just wished he didn't find her so physically attractive. His body reacted to her nearness like a Geiger counter in the presence of radioactivity. All systems started flashing *go*, refusing to understand the reality of their situation.

He would have to concentrate on the task at hand—first, find transportation; second, escort Melanie to her friend's home. It might even help to keep in mind that he was having lustful thoughts toward his closest friend's sister-in-law. Whatever occurred down here, he would have to explain it to Damon—and possibly Elise.

He had been sent to find and protect Melanie, not to seduce her.

A very faint light seeped into Melanie's room the next morning, just enough to create darker shadows where the sparse furniture was located.

Justin shook her shoulder and whispered. "Melanie, we've got to get out of here."

Startled, she rolled over and sat up. "How did you get in here?"

"Crawled through the window. Look, we don't have any time to waste. We've got to get out of here," he repeated.

"Why?"

He grabbed her suitcase and dumped its contents out on the bed, ignoring her question. "Find something to wear and grab what you absolutely cannot live without and put it in my backpack." He picked up that article and tossed it on the bed, as well.

Since the bed was rather narrow, Melanie was now almost completely covered with her clothes and his pack. "What in the world's the matter with you? You act like someone's after us."

"Not yet, but if they knew we were here, they certainly would be." He tugged on her hands until she was forced to stand up beside the bed. "We've got about another fifteen minutes before sunrise. Let's try to be out of here by then." He opened the door.

"Where are you going?"

"To find something to eat. I'll leave your hostess plenty of money to pay for it, but we're going to have to get lost for a while."

She shook her head in bewilderment. Melanie wasn't much of a morning person to begin with, but trying to make sense out of what was happening was creating more difficulties than usual.

By the time she had dressed and packed, Melanie was enough awake to want some answers. She was just finishing braiding her hair when Justin slipped into the room. If she hadn't been facing the door, she wouldn't have known he was there.

"Would you please tell me what is going on?"

"Not now. Let's get away from here. I'll explain later."

He peeked out the window. No one was stirring. Grabbing his backpack, he eased it down on the ground outside, crawled out, then turned around and held out his arms.

"C'mon," he whispered.

All right, you wanted adventure in your life, didn't you? You wanted a little excitement? Well...here goes!

Taking a deep breath, Melanie crawled out of the window and into Justin's arms.

It took all her concentration to keep up with him. Justin had skirted the town to reach the other side, rather than walking through it. No one was stirring and Melanie could not understand the need for all the stealth and secrecy, but she went along with it. There was nothing much she could do about it.

Justin found a path away from the village and the road they had intended to take.

"Where are we going?"

"We're going to hide in the jungle for a day or two, until I'm certain it's safe to show our faces."

They hiked for several hours, stopping for short breaks for water and to catch their breaths. From the grim expression on Justin's face, the situation was serious.

Eventually they came to a small clearing and Justin decided they would stop for lunch. Melanie's legs were crying out for rest. She considered herself to be in good shape, but the uneven terrain and the need for speed had placed additional strain on her that she wasn't prepared for.

"Who are we running from?"

They were stretched out in the clearing eating the chicken and rolls Justin had found in Rosa's kitchen.

"His name is Victor Degas and he's one mean dude, let me tell you."

"How do you know him?"

"Several years ago, when I was young and idealistic, I was involved in some undercover narcotics work for the U.S. government." He glanced over at Melanie. "I don't know if you are aware, but Colombia has the biggest cocaine traffic in this hemisphere."

"Of course I know that. I watch *Miami Vice* every Friday night!"

"What are you talking about?"

"Oh, never mind. I forgot you've been down here for so long. Is Victor Degas one of the smugglers?"

"Yes. I managed to work my way into his organization. It took us years to get set up, but eventually I was one of his most trusted people."

"And—"

"And I was able to blow his entire operations on both continents. Unfortunately he wriggled loose from the net and escaped."

"Does he know you were the one who caused it to happen?"

"Who knows? I never came back to find out. And I don't have any desire to find out now."

"What do you think he would have done if he'd seen you?"

"Victor has a habit of shooting first, and if you're still alive, asking a few questions afterward."

"And Victor was in the village?"

"Yes. I think he and his men were going to Bogotá and had to turn back because of the mud slide. So they stopped at the village late last night to find rooms."

"Did he see you?"

"No. I was in the other room when they came in, but I recognized his voice immediately. I waited until after they'd eaten and gone to bed before I came to get you."

She studied him for a few minutes in silence. "I had no idea that you led such an exciting life."

He laughed. "That's one way of looking at it, but it was a long time ago."

"How old are you?"

"Thirty-seven."

"And you've never been married?"

"How can you tell?"

"I'm not sure. You give the impression that you've never stayed in one place long enough to acquire a wife, much less a family."

"That's a fairly accurate assessment."

"Does Damon know about your past?"

"Of course."

"Is that why he contacted you to come after me?"

He nodded. "However, it looks like you would have been safer on your own than with me." He glanced around the clearing and stood up. "I spent the hours while I waited for Victor to go to bed thinking about what I should do about you. If Julio had still been there, I would have left you. But I couldn't go off and leave you alone, without speaking the language.

"Besides, Victor has a weakness for blondes. If he had heard that you were there, he would have torn up the village to find you. And Victor isn't very kind to his lady friends."

She shivered. She was glad Justin had decided to take her with him. Taking the hand Justin offered her, she pulled herself up to stand beside him. "I've al-

ways wanted some adventure in my life. Now's my
chance!'' She grinned up at him with such a look of
excitement and expectation that he almost groaned.

She had no idea what might be in store for them,
and he didn't have the heart to explain. Maybe she
would never need to know men such as Victor Degas,
nor about their sadistic practices and depraved life-
styles.

He'd do everything in his power to protect her from
them.

Melanie had never seen anything so wonderful in
her life than the three tiny buildings clustered together in a small clearing. Although it had only been
a few hours, she had followed Justin for what seemed
like days through dense undergrowth. She had never
expected to see quite so much of Colombia and
couldn't help but reflect on how her plans had gone
awry.

*But if I were to plan to be marooned with anyone, I
couldn't choose anyone I'd rather be with than Justin,* she honestly admitted to herself. Their hours together were a far cry from the civilized life she was
used to, but she had been looking for some excitement and adventure. Now she had found it. No one
had told her that excitement and adventure could be
very tough on the feet.

At least they had finally found other people in the
wilderness. Justin stopped only long enough to remove his backpack, then strode to the nearest dwell-
ing. Within minutes the clearing seemed to be

swarming with men, women, children, barking dogs and assorted barnyard animals.

She watched Justin as he spoke, his hands periodically gesturing in some sort of explanation. At one point all those gathered around him turned to look at her, then back at him and his conversation. Eventually everyone nodded, and he returned to her side.

"I think we're in luck," he began.

"Fantastic. They're going to show us to the local Hilton."

"Not that much luck, I'm afraid."

She shrugged. "It doesn't matter. A comfortable Holiday Inn would do."

"They're going to give us a bed for the night, and one of them has a Jeep that they're willing to use to get us to the next town."

"You mean to tell me there's a road around here, and we've missed it?"

"From what they tell me the road is on the other side of the settlement, but I for one have done all the traveling I intend to do in one day." He leaned over and picked up his gear with one hand, took her hand with his other one and led her to the village.

"Do you suppose they have anything resembling a shower?"

"We'll find out."

They did. As a matter of fact, the villagers were quite pleased with their bathing facilities. A couple of the men led them along a well-trodden path to a stream that produced a small water fall and miniscule pool. They smiled and gestured, and Melanie tried to suppress a groan. But it was much better than nothing. She waited patiently until the other men left, then turned to Justin.

"Shall we draw straws as to who goes first?"

"No need. There's room for both of us." He sat down beside the stream and began to unfasten his laced boots. Melanie watched him with growing alarm when he pulled off his boots and stood up, quickly hauling his shirt over his head and unfastening his pants.

"Wait a minute, Justin. We can't bathe together!"

His hands paused just as his pants were low around his hips. "Why not?"

"Well," she blustered. "Just because we can't, that's why!"

"Melanie," he said in a patient voice, "I recognize that this isn't the way we'd do it back in the States, but the point is, we aren't *in* the States right now. I'm not trying to embarrass you or cause you to feel shame. There is absolutely nothing wrong with our bathing together. The Japanese have been doing it for years. We don't want to be out here after dark, and there isn't time to bathe separately before the sun sets." He grinned at her, a boyish grin that poked gentle fun at her protests. "I'm afraid I'm just not enough of a gentleman to do without a bath in order to preserve your modesty. Besides, whether you like it or not, I've already seen all you have to offer."

Justin completed the motion his hands had started earlier and removed his pants, stepping out of them with complete unconcern.

Melanie considered herself to be a mature, well-educated, modern woman. It just so happened that she had never seen an adult male without clothes on before. There was a tremendous difference in the physique of a thirty-seven-year-old male and her five-year-old nephew!

Justin stepped into the stream as though he were alone, having paused only long enough to palm the bar of soap he had brought in his backpack. Melanie felt frozen into place as her gaze took in the broad width of his shoulders, the rippling muscles along his back, the firm tautness of his buttocks—several shades lighter than the rest of him—and the long, muscular length of his legs.

She forced herself to swallow, then looked down at her hands clenched together. He was right. There was no reason to panic. If she wanted to crawl out of her self-imposed rut, she needed to be open to new experiences. There was no reason for her to act like some screaming, shrinking virgin. She refused to accept either adjective to describe herself, but could not deny the noun.

Not that she had any intention of broadcasting the condition. The best way to handle the matter was calmly, as though she was used to bathing with a man. As nonchalantly as possible, Melanie began to disrobe.

Justin watched her out of the corner of his eye, doing everything in his power not to grin at her obvious discomfort. He had been proud of her today. She really had not been in any condition to be moving at such a pace for an extended period of time, but she had kept up with him without complaint. Never once had she pointed out that she would have preferred to stay in the village and take her chances, nor had she pointed out that so far the only danger she had been exposed to since arriving in Colombia had come because of him!

He tried not to think about it, but his mind kept returning to the knotty problem of Victor and what to do about him. Justin couldn't help but wonder what the hell he was doing in this district. Victor's stomping grounds were generally around the coast and Cartagena. *Wouldn't you know he'd happen to be passing through this area at the same time I'm here,* he thought with irritation.

He would do whatever necessary to protect Melanie.

Melanie. He glanced around as she was shyly stepping out of her jeans, looking in every direction but his. He wondered if she intended to wear her bra and bikini briefs into the water—obviously she was thinking about it. With a hint of defiance in the angle of her head, she reached back and unsnapped her bra. God, she was beautiful! With economical movements she stepped out of her panties and gingerly walked into the water.

Justin closed his eyes and began to scrub himself, trying to dismiss the image of her lovely body coming toward him completely unadorned.

The water felt refreshing, and Melanie was pleased she hadn't chosen to stay on the side. The small pool barely came to her hips and she knelt down, hoping for more modest cover. Justin had walked under the waterfall, letting the sluice of liquid rinse his body of soap.

"Here, catch!" he called, and she glanced up in time to see the soap sailing through the air. She laughed, grabbing it.

"Great catch," he commented.

"Great throw," she acknowledged.

They grinned at each other, and she realized that she was getting accustomed to the sight of his body. He seemed to be totally unaware of their lack of clothing, and she was determined to ignore the fact, as well.

Melanie was forced to remind herself of her new-found sophistication a few hours later. As the evening progressed she found herself more and more in need of it.

Justin patiently explained they were fortunate to find *any* place to sleep, and since one of the couples had generously given up their bed to them, he wasn't about to demand another one just because of her ridiculous scruples.

"They aren't ridiculous, Justin. I just don't think it's a very good idea for us to sleep together."

"I'm not exactly doing handsprings myself, Melanie. So what do you suggest we do?" Before she had a chance to speak he added, "And don't tell me I can sleep outside. I told you before I'm not that much of a gentleman."

She grinned at his irritated tone and expression. He had really been pushed that day. And after all, what was wrong with them sharing a bed? It wasn't as though they were strangers. In fact she probably knew more about Justin than she knew about any other man.

The trouble with Melanie was that she had never been around many men. Her dad had died when she was still a child. Her brother had married and moved away from home when she was still quite young, and she had been too busy with first school, and then her shop, to spend much time with anyone other than Philip. Unfortunately Philip's conversation could put her to sleep in fifteen minutes. She had never been tempted or aroused by him and had therefore concluded that she just wasn't interested in the physical aspect of a relationship.

Now she had to rethink all of her previous opinions. Melanie was far from comfortable with the feelings that Justin stirred up in her, and she didn't know what to do about them. But she had a strong hunch that sleeping next to him would not make them go away.

For a moment she wondered if she was still dreaming, still lying in the village in a fevered state of hallucination. Nothing had seemed real to her since Justin had appeared.

"All right," she eventually said with obvious reluctance. "I'll sleep with you."

"Your enthusiasm does great things for my ego, let me tell you."

"I don't think anything could dent your ego."

"Ouch. You definitely have a way with words."

One of the villagers spoke to Justin in a rapid tone that sounded more like machine gun fire than a foreign language. Melanie shook her head. She was really lost when it came to understanding the natives.

Justin turned back to her. "He said we could join them for something to eat, which sounds fine to me. How about you?"

Melanie nodded. She was ready to eat and get some rest. Hopefully by the next morning, most of their problems would be over. They would have a ride to the next village, then could find transportation on into the interior.

Later that evening Melanie discovered it took no effort at all for her to curl up with her head on Justin's shoulder. As both of them were fully clothed, the situation seemed decorous and even somewhat reassuring. She promptly fell asleep.

Justin lay there for several hours, listening to her even breathing, feeling the warmth of her body in the heat of the night. He sighed. Could this be some sort of punishment because of the unfettered life he had lived? The women he'd known had all understood the rules and been eager to spend whatever time with him he had available.

He wasn't used to denying himself.

Closing his eyes with new resolve, Justin decided he was going to have to practice a great deal of denial before this trip was completed.

Their sleep was rudely interrupted a few hours later by a harsh, guttural voice speaking heavily accented English.

"Welcome back to Colombia, Señor Drake. If you'd only let me know you were coming, I would have had a much nicer welcome prepared."

Melanie jerked up in alarm, her heart pounding. The small hut seemed to be full of people, all holding lethal-looking automatic rifles. One of them had a large flashlight trained on them, the glare almost blinding them, causing their visitors to appear more like silhouettes and shadows surrounding them than real people.

Justin leaned up on one elbow and casually raked his hand through his hair. "Well, hello, Victor. What a surprise—seeing you again after all these years."

Three

———

Come with me, amigo, I'm sure we can find you much better accommodations than these," Victor said with a sneer. He prodded Justin with a booted foot. "Get up." His voice held a menacing quality that did nothing to soothe Melanie's anxiety. This must be the man Justin had wanted to avoid, for regardless of what he had called Justin, she knew he was no friend. He made her skin crawl.

With slow, deliberate movements Justin sat up, keeping his hands visible. After he was on his feet he turned and offered his hand to Melanie.

"I'm surprised to see you traveling with a woman. I remember you as a loner," Victor commented. "I suppose you're sniffing out some more contacts down here, eh?''

"My reasons for being in Colombia are personal, not professional, Victor," Justin said in a level voice.

"So you say, but I have reason not to believe you."

"I've never lied to you."

"No? Perhaps that is so. But perhaps you feel pretending to be in the trade was not a lie."

"There was no pretense."

"But isn't it interesting that when our base was discovered by the authorities you were conveniently away."

"So?"

"So it is my belief that after you managed to weasel your way into my operation, you turned us in and got out in time to save your neck."

"Talk sense, Victor. Why would I turn you in? I had much more to gain by staying with your organization."

"Very true. But your disappearance was a little too timely. And I never heard from you again."

"When I heard what happened at the camp, I knew better than to return. I wasn't sure who had turned traitor, who I could trust. As far as I knew, *you* had reported the operation."

The Colombian threw back his head and laughed, then abruptly stopped. "Let's go, Drake. I'm willing to give you the benefit of the doubt at the moment. In other words, I'm going to let you live long enough to prove what you say is true." He jerked his head toward the opening of the hut. "Come."

Justin kept Melanie close to his side while Victor and his men led them through the small clearing and down a path that wound through the jungle. Melanie could scarcely see. Occasionally one of them would flash a beam of light on some obstacle in the path, then the light would be gone. Justin seemed to have no trouble seeing in the dark. She was glad he kept her close to his side.

When they came out on a road of sorts, Victor motioned for them to climb into the first Jeep that was parked along the road. The other men climbed into a second one.

"How did you find us?" Justin asked in a casual tone once they were moving along the narrow road.

"The village was full of talk about the beautiful blond *norteamericano* and her so tall and handsome husband. I wanted to know who you were and why you were here, so I followed you. I'm glad I did. It was just good fortune that my curiosity caused me to find out more about you."

"So you didn't know it was me."

"Not until I found you, no. As I said, it was my good fortune."

Justin sat in the back seat of the Jeep with his arm around Melanie, continuing to hold her closely to his side. The driver didn't seem to care about the lack of visibility and the rough road. He sped around the curves as though in a race. If it hadn't been for Justin she would have been thrown out more than once.

"So when did you decide to marry, Drake?" Victor asked in Spanish after several miles of silence.

"What difference does it make?" Justin replied in the same language.

"No difference. I just wondered. I never saw you as the type to settle down."

"Everyone changes as he grows older."

"Particularly when he finds one such as yours, eh? She seems a little young for you ... and a little innocent for my taste."

"But I didn't choose her to please your taste."

Victor laughed. "True. Of course I might be willing to take her off your hands if you grow tired of her. No doubt she could be taught to please."

Justin glanced down to see if Melanie was following the conversation. He wished there was some way he could reassure her that everything was going to be all right. Unfortunately the situation was far from all right. The fact that he was still alive actually surprised him. Maybe Victor had grown softer in the years since they had worked together. Either that or there was a very real doubt in Victor's mind who had betrayed him.

Justin hoped he could fan that doubt into a flame that might save his life.

He tried not to think of what could happen to Melanie if Victor decided to get rid of him. Justin was relieved to know his tracks had been covered enough to leave a doubt as to his involvement with the cocaine operation and its eventual exposure. It was sheer bad luck that their paths should cross now.

"Where are we going?" He hoped he sounded casual enough.

"To my place."

"My wife and I are on our way to Villa Vicencias to visit with a school friend of hers. She is going to be worried when we don't arrive."

"What were you doing in the village back there?"

"Trying to find transportation. We got caught in the mud slide that closed off the highway to Bogotá."

He sincerely hoped no one in the village had thought to mention to Victor that Justin had arrived a few days after Melanie. He waited tensely for Victor's response but there was none. He could only hope Victor had bought his story.

"Where are we going?" Melanie murmured softly, her mouth pressed against his ear.

Justin had been trying to ignore the warmth of the woman pressed against his side, her fragrance wafting around him as a constant reminder. The touch of her mouth against his ear caused his blood to race and he took a deep breath, trying to control his reaction.

He turned his head, his lips brushing softly against hers. Slowly continuing his journey to her ear, he whispered his answer. "Victor is taking us to his headquarters."

"Why?" she whispered.

He shook his head slightly, then squeezed her hand gently, hoping to convey a sense of security that was sadly lacking in their situation. Placing her hand on his thigh, he stroked it lightly, hoping the touch might help her to relax.

"We'll talk later," he promised softly, glancing at the two men sitting in front to see if they were listening.

Melanie felt protected by Justin's presence. Beneath the palm of her hand she could feel the muscled strength of his thigh, its tenseness communicating his wariness in the present situation. He had one arm around her shoulders, while his other hand stroked her knuckles and fingers, back and forth, over and over, in a gentle, rhythmic motion that was almost hypnotic.

It seemed to Melanie that every situation they encountered caused them to draw closer together physically, which played havoc with her peace of mind.

How much longer were they going to have to pretend to be a couple? She stared at the man who had issued his "invitation" accompanied by automatic rifles. There was a faint possibility that the natives of South America expressed their hospitality in that manner. If so, Stephen Birnbaum had forgotten to mention it in his latest travel guide. Somehow, Melanie felt Victor followed his own, rather brutal, rules of behavior that wouldn't be found in any guidebook.

After several miles they turned onto a road that was barely a trail. Long vines and tree limbs slapped at them as they rode along. At least the two men in front had some protection from the windshield, Melanie thought with dismay. She and Justin couldn't dodge the foliage fast enough before it hit them.

Justin swore and jerked her even closer to him, forcing her face into his chest. "Dammit, Victor, have your driver slow down, will you?"

Victor glanced over his shoulder and noting their predicament, rapped out an order to the driver, who immediately slowed.

"Sorry, amigo."

I just bet you are, Justin thought. He recognized the slight smile on Victor's face. It always reminded him of the complacent cat who could give no clue as to the whereabouts of the family canary, nor explain the feathers that surrounded him. *I'm too old for this life,* Justin reluctantly admitted to himself. *And I've been away from it too long.*

As if to contradict the thought, his senses continued to sharpen as the trail wound its way through the underbrush. He noted the other tracks leading off it and made mental note of distinctive landmarks. His ability to get them out of there rapidly could mean the difference between life and death.

When the Jeep came to an abrupt halt, both Justin and Melanie braced themselves to keep from hitting the back of the front seats.

"Welcome to my home, Drake," Victor said expansively as he crawled out of the front seat. "Let's go inside."

There were no yard lights, and the place was ghostly silent. Justin knew they were being watched by Victor's hidden men. He carefully crawled out of the Jeep and turned to assist Melanie.

Victor walked to her other side and gestured. "As you can see, I keep a quiet place here."

Justin nodded. He didn't like the feel of the place. Not at all. But there wasn't a hell of a lot he could do about it. He draped his arm across Melanie's shoulders and followed Victor into the house.

Once inside, Victor turned on lights that brought the interior of the large house into sharp focus. The entryway was covered with red Spanish tile and the white walls stretched upward to a second story. A balcony with wrought-iron railing surrounded the upper level.

Victor started up the stairway. "We might as well get some sleep." He paused at the second door on the upper balcony, pushing it open. "I'll talk with you in the morning." He waited for them to enter and once they did, he closed the door. The click of the lock was clearly audible to the two remaining in the room.

Melanie watched as Justin inspected their new quarters. He disappeared into the bathroom and came out shortly with an amused look on his face.

"All the comforts of home. This certainly beats the accommodations we were just forced to vacate." He walked over to where she stood staring uncertainly around the room.

"Somehow I felt safer at the other place," she finally admitted.

He chuckled, drawing her into his arms. "I'm so sorry this happened, Melanie."

"You can't blame yourself. You did your best to keep out of his way."

"I underestimated him. A mistake like that could easily have been fatal."

She rested her head on his chest. "So what do we do now?"

He massaged the stiffness in her neck and shoulders, kneading them until he felt the tension drain away. "We try to get some sleep."

Melanie raised her head to stare at the imposing bed dominating the room. Sharing a luxurious bedroom seemed to be much more intimate than sharing the little hut they had previously occupied. She looked up at him, her expression carefully blank.

"You didn't have any trouble going to sleep with me before," he pointed out in a reasonable voice. "Why should this be any different? We'll have considerably more room."

She could feel the heavy thudding of his heart and for just a moment allowed herself the luxury of relaxing against him once more.

Everything was happening too fast between them. She knew it and he knew it, she was sure. Perhaps he felt it was better to ignore the tension that had been building between them since he had first walked into her room. Had that only been three days ago? It seemed like they had been together for weeks, even months.

She only felt safe when they were touching. But whenever he touched her a vibration began deep inside her that convinced her she would never be safe around him. Yet the feelings were different. With him beside her, she felt safe from harm. With him beside her, she no longer felt safe from the churning emotions his presence stirred within her.

For the first time in her life, Melanie felt a strong desire to make love to a man. No matter how hard she denied her feelings, they wouldn't go away. But she knew she mustn't give in to them.

Justin stepped back from her. "I think I'll go take a shower." *A very cold shower,* he added to himself. "Then you can have the bathroom to yourself."

He walked into the other room and closed the door.

Melanie dug through the backpack and found her nightgown. She might as well sleep as comfortably as possible, she decided. Then she paused. Wasn't that inviting his attention?

What if it was?

She was afraid to face the answer to that question.

If only Justin didn't appeal to her in so many different ways. She couldn't have found a more considerate companion. He hadn't made an issue of his knowledge or his need to lead. He hadn't bullied or chastised her. He had simply done what was necessary without making her feel she had no choice in the matter.

That was it! She never felt stifled around him. He accepted her for who she was and made no demands on her. He allowed her to be free, but was there to protect her from harm.

In other words, Justin Drake fit the description every female carried around of the perfect knight in shining armor, even to coming to the rescue of a damsel in distress.

It was no wonder she found herself falling in love with him.

The sound of the bathroom door opening drew her attention and Melanie looked around. Justin had put on a clean pair of jeans, no doubt to appease her modesty. He hadn't bothered with a shirt or shoes. Melanie couldn't force her eyes from the view. His wide chest was heavily muscled. The nipples were surrounded by a soft mat of blond hair that formed a V at his waist, then became a narrow line disappearing beneath the low hung jeans whose button remained open.

"It's all yours," he said quietly.

His low-voiced statement caused an electrical jolt to shoot through her before she realized he was referring to the bathroom.

Refusing to meet his gaze, Melanie grabbed her gown and started to walk past him.

He stopped her by gently touching her cheek. "What's wrong?" he asked, a puzzled expression replacing his earlier look of relaxation.

Hesitantly she met his gaze. His eyes were glowing—a deep, rich blue flame that seemed to pull her, mothlike, ever closer. She was afraid of the message in them. She had been fighting her reactions to him, somehow maintaining a semblance of control. But she knew she couldn't fight both of them—and win.

She shook her head slightly. "I'm just tired—and a little frightened. This has been a little more adventure than I was quite ready for."

He cupped her chin in his hand. "I know. And you've handled it very well. I'm extremely proud of you." He leaned over and kissed her nose, then dropped his hand. "Enjoy your bath. There seems to be plenty of hot water." *There should be. I used damned little of it!*

He watched her go into the bathroom and close the door, then wandered over to one of the long, narrow windows and stared out into the warm night. Wrought-iron bars guarded the windows, but he had noted those details earlier. He could see nothing outside—the soft light of the room reflected off the glass, giving him a duplicate image of the bedroom.

He wished to hell there *was* another bedroom, but he didn't dare let Victor realize he and Melanie weren't married. Their imaginary relationship was the only protection he could give her at the moment. The question that had begun to eat at him was: who was going to protect her from him?

Turning back to the room, he walked over to the door and flipped off the light. Only a faint strip of illumination from beneath the bathroom door gave him enough light to find his way to the bed.

He drew the covers back, then unzipped his jeans and let them fall to the floor. He stepped out of them and stretched out on the bed, surprised to discover how comfortable it was. Victor had not spared any expense. Being given such a well-turned-out room was a good sign. Other than having the door locked on them, they were being treated more as guests than prisoners.

As hard as he tried to keep his mind on ways to get away from Victor, Justin's traitorous thoughts kept returning to Melanie—Melanie of the laughing face, the sparkling eyes, the mischievous grin, the oh-so-kissable mouth. He groaned. Would he ever forget how she had looked earlier, carefully stepping into the small stream? Her slenderness emphasized her high, firm breasts; her tiny waist flared gracefully into her hips and thighs. Everything about her was symmetrical. She could have posed for a sculptor.

The thought of another man seeing her as he had caused a tightness in his chest. A surge of possessiveness surged through him.

Damn! He didn't want another man to see her. He didn't want another man to know how it felt to kiss her, to feel her body pressed closely to his.

Then it hit him. The pretense had become very real to him. He wanted her, all right. He wanted her in every way a man could want a woman. He wanted her as his wife.

He lay there feeling as though a giant tree had fallen on him. He, Justin Drake, wanted to marry Melanie Montgomery.

"I must be out of my mind," he muttered under his breath.

Marry Elise Trent's baby sister? The family would never allow it. Let her move off to South America to live? Not on your life!

But she did say she had always wanted to visit Buenos Aires.

Visit, not move there.

Maybe she would like it. She's looking for something different in life.

She *was*. After this little trip, if they managed to get out alive, she'd be more than ready to settle down in her hometown and never budge.

I could always ask her. Give her the choice.

And have her laugh in your face? Or point out how she's been trying to be independent—and marriage isn't on her agenda?

Being married to me wouldn't have to stop her from being independent.

Try telling her that.

I will!

Feeling as though he'd just won the most important argument of his life, Justin fell asleep, a slight smile on his face.

Melanie couldn't believe her luck. She found some bath oil in a bottle stored beneath the sink. After filling the oversize tub to capacity with steamy water liberally sprinkled with bath oil, she eased herself into the tub, sighing with pleasure.

Never before had she fully appreciated the luxury of a hot bath. She knew she would never take one for granted again.

She wondered what Justin was doing in the other room. He probably had crawled into bed and promptly fallen asleep. Of course that was what she wanted him to do, wasn't it? She suddenly remembered the warm look in his eyes just before she had come in to run her bath water. She shivered. It had probably been a trick of the lighting.

He had been treating her as though she *had* dreamed the kiss they had shared. Perhaps she did. He could have come into the room and left and her imagination could have made up the rest.

But it had seemed so real!

Since then he'd been kind and considerate of her, but treated her as though he was only a family friend.

I want to be so much more to him, she realized with a pang. As unpredictable as their present situation was, she was glad they were there together. What if he had gone off and left her by herself? She would never have had this time with him. She didn't care how long they had to stay as long as eventually they were allowed to leave unharmed.

Perhaps Justin would get used to having her around. She smiled at the thought. He was just as independent as she was, so she knew how much he needed his space. The one thing she already knew about him was that he wouldn't tolerate a possessive woman. Her smile grew wider. For the first time in her life Melanie had found someone worth giving up some of her independence for. All she had to do was convince him that she was what *he* needed.

Melanie lost track of time but the cooling water finally began to impinge on her consciousness. She reluctantly got out of the tub and grabbed the large bath towel hanging nearby. After vigorously drying herself she slipped on her gown, then brushed the tangles from her hair.

Recognizing her reluctance to face Justin, she forced herself to open the door and walk into the bedroom. Justin had turned out the light and was obviously asleep. He lay with his back to her on the far edge of the bed, making it clear he did not intend to crowd her.

Snapping off the bathroom light, she carefully felt her way to the bed. After slipping between the smooth sheets, she pulled the covers high over her shoulders. The combination of the warm water and the comfortable bed soon lulled her into a deep, restful sleep.

Sometime during the night the vast distance that had originally separated Justin and Melanie lessened. By morning she was curled up next to his side, her head on his shoulder, his chin resting against her hair. Her arm was draped across his chest and her knee had also found a very comfortable nest—it was securely nestled near a very private part of Justin's anatomy.

They both continued to sleep soundly, comfortably enjoying their dreams—their extraordinarily sensuous dreams.

Melanie's gown had inched its way up until it was gathered around her thighs, and when Justin's hand slid down the smooth length of her back, his gesture seemed to be a part of both of their dreams.

Slowly but surely he found the soft curve of her bare hip, and he lazily stroked from her waist to her thigh, then casually moved upward once more.

Melanie shifted restlessly beneath his touch. In her dream her bones seemed to have turned to mush and her body felt too heavy to move.

She turned her head and Justin slid his hand along her shoulder and up to her neck, where he gently turned her mouth toward his. He nibbled, pulling at her lower lip, teasing her with his tongue, slowly exploring the shape of her mouth, fitting his lips to the shape of hers.

Yes! This was the kiss she remembered! This was the marvelous way she had felt. No other man had ever made her feel that way.

Melanie's mouth blossomed like a flower bud unfurling itself in the morning sunlight and Justin increased his possession of her mouth. His tongue explored with increasing intimacy and daring, and Melanie responded to him with a warm burst of desire.

Justin shifted his position on the bed, rolling more fully onto his back so that Melanie lay intimately pressed against his long, muscled length, their mouths fused in a passionate interlocking.

Her breasts pressed tightly against his broad chest, the thin lace of her gown offering little resistance between them. Justin's hands freely stroked her back, from her neck down to her legs, lovingly caressing her curves.

Their dreams suddenly coalesced into passionate reality, the transition so natural they were both caught up in the emotional whirlpool before they were fully aware of their actions.

Melanie became aware of his arousal, hard against her abdomen, and felt a sudden exhilaration that she had caused such a strong reaction.

Her hands slipped through his hair and she luxuriated in the feel of the thick, tawny mane that framed his face, her mouth never leaving his.

So this is what it feels like to make love. Her body had taken over instinctively, and her hips moved provocatively against him.

With a sudden surge of power Justin rolled over so that Melanie was lying on the bed. Bending over her he pressed his lips against her breasts that were revealed to him, kissing them, teasing the nipples with his tongue.

His hands had not been still, but had circled and explored her waist, her abdomen, her thighs. There was one spot he seemed to miss, one area that Melanie found herself wanting him to touch. She moaned in frustration.

The sound seemed to break through his control. His mouth found hers once more at the same time his hand found the place that desperately needed appeasing. She sighed with the pleasure of his touch, his tongue and fingers producing a rhythm that was rapidly reducing Melanie to a quivering mass of mindless sensation.

Her hands clutched his shoulders, and she desperately wanted to share the indescribable sensations he was creating—

"Am I interrupting something?"

Justin and Melanie froze in their intimate position. Justin raised his head. Melanie's eyes flew open. She absently noted his flushed cheeks, and the dark blaze of passion in his eyes. Then he rolled away from her, making sure the covers never revealed any part of her to their unwelcome visitor.

Justin came up on one elbow, ruthlessly raking his hair away from his face. He glared at the grinning man who stood just inside the open door. Justin mentally cursed himself for being too involved with Melanie to hear the door being unlocked. He forced himself to calm down. Too many emotions were still fighting for control. He couldn't allow himself to put them into any more danger than they already were.

"You've got the damnedest timing, Victor," he said, shaking his head ruefully.

Melanie was trembling so hard she could barely hold the covers in place. She stared at the man who had entered their room unnoticed. His malicious smile made her skin crawl. He looked almost disappointed that they had stopped what they were doing when he spoke!

"Do you have something against knocking?" Justin asked when Victor gave no sign of commenting to his last remark.

"No, but I don't waste my time with unimportant details, although I admit I was surprised to see you so actively engaged this early in the morning. Marriage must have changed your old habits."

Justin rolled out of bed and stood, his tall, lean frame several inches taller than the other man's. "Let's leave my habits out of this, if you don't mind." He leaned over and picked up his jeans. Stepping into them with economical movements, he zipped them and said, "What do you want, now that you're here?"

Victor laughed. "Perhaps I should allow you to finish what you started, amigo. We could all benefit from a friendlier mood from you."

"Look, Victor. I appreciate your hospitality, but we need to be going. As long as you felt it was necessary to come in here at this time, I don't suppose it's too much to ask that you provide us with some sort of transportation so we can get on to Villa Vicencias."

"Ah, but it was that very subject that I came here to discuss."

Justin casually glanced at Melanie and wished he hadn't. Her flushed cheeks and tousled hair were a needless reminder of what had so nearly happened earlier—what he wished *had* happened. He knew this was her first time. To have it so traumatically interrupted might create an emotional scar no one could ever remove.

He glanced back to Victor. "Is there someplace else we can talk? Melanie needs some privacy to dress."

Victor grinned. "No problem." He motioned to the open doorway. "My office is downstairs. We have several things that need to be discussed." His gaze returned to the woman in bed. "I'll see you later, Señora Drake."

Justin followed Victor out the door, then paused. "I'll be down in a moment," he said to Victor.

Without waiting for Victor's comment, he shut the door and walked back toward the bed. Victor's laugh echoed in the wide expanse of the balcony, stairwell and foyer.

"What a horrible man," Melanie muttered, her eyes refusing to meet Justin's.

He sat down on the side of the bed and took her hand. It was icy cold, and she was trembling.

"Yes, he is. I'll never forgive myself for allowing him to upset you like this."

Her green gaze flew to him in surprise. "It wasn't your fault he came bursting in like that!"

"No, but it was my fault for starting something we couldn't properly finish."

Her lashes fell, effectively masking her eyes. "That wasn't your fault, either."

"Oh, wasn't it?" He grinned. "Then that only leaves one other person." He gently stroked her hand, grateful to feel the warmth returning.

"Well, I, uh, you see..." She refused to look at him, but she hadn't removed her hand from his.

He laughed, delighted with her confusion, relieved she wasn't in tears or hurling accusations at him. Perhaps there wouldn't be any scars.

"Melanie, look at me." He waited until her gaze met his. "What almost happened between us—what is definitely going to happen between us soon—was inevitable. I've wanted to make love to you since I walked into your room and you greeted me with total nonchalance at my sudden appearance. If the truth were known, I've wanted you even longer than that—since I first met the fascinating schoolgirl with the flashing emerald eyes."

She began to relax and a smile teased around the edges of her mouth.

"I'm sorrier than I can say that our first time together had to end so abruptly. Will you forgive me?"

"Of course." Her voice was so low he could scarcely hear it.

"I'm glad." He patted her hand, then stood up. "I've got to talk to Victor and get us out of here." His sudden smile was devastating. "We've got some unfinished business to take care of." He leaned over and gave her a short but very thorough and possessive kiss.

He opened the door, then glanced over his shoulder. In a very casual voice he said, "Did I remember to mention to you that I happen to love you very much?"

The door closed quietly behind him.

Melanie gazed at the door as though in a trance. She couldn't believe what she had just heard. But had she ever known Justin to lie?

Her body still throbbed from his lovemaking. The interruption had been like waking up in the middle of a marvelous dream. But no dream could compare to the reality of Justin's lovemaking.

And he loved her. She had a hunch that having Justin love her would provide all the excitement and adventure she would ever need.

Four

Justin left the bedroom and strode down the winding staircase. A young man wearing a pistol in a shoulder holster waited at the bottom. When Justin reached him the man nodded his head toward a closed door on the main floor.

Justin opened the door and stepped inside. An arsenal of guns and rifles, many of them automatic, hung along one of the walls. Various-sized maps covered another one. Victor sat behind a mammoth desk watching him, his boots propped on the scarred desktop.

Waving his hand negligently, Victor said, "Sit down, Drake. We have some catching up to do." He leaned over and picked up a box of cigars, flipped it open and offered them to Justin.

Justin shook his head. Victor shrugged, helped himself to one and for the next few minutes made a production out of snipping off one end, lighting it and puffing on the cigar until it was lit to his satisfaction. Justin recognized the ploy for what it was. If Justin had anything to be nervous about, Victor's delaying tactics should increase the nervousness until he gave something of his feelings of unease away.

However, Justin had been at the game a long time. He recognized the tactic for what it was and refused to fall for it. Instead he waited for Victor's next move.

"How long has it been, amigo?" His black eyes gave away nothing of his thoughts.

Justin stretched his legs out in front of him, crossing them at the ankles. "About ten years, I'd say." He allowed himself a slight smile. "You haven't changed much, have you?"

"What do you mean?"

Justin gestured to the room in general. "You seem to be prospering."

Victor nodded. "But it has taken many years for me to rebuild what I lost on the coast."

"This place shows considerable flair and style. I was surprised. Your place on the coast wasn't half so grand."

Victor shrugged. He puffed on his cigar, then removed it from his mouth, slowly blowing smoke rings. "I had a little help. The man who built this place suddenly decided Colombia was not a healthy place to live, so he left it for me."

Reading the message in Victor's eyes Justin had a hunch the original owner never made it out of the country.

"I couldn't see much of the place last night, but it looks quite impressive."

"I cleared an area nearby for an airstrip, something I never needed on the coast."

"So you're in the same business."

"But of course. It's a very profitable one, so long as I trust no one but myself."

"You have no reason not to trust me, Victor."

"You still insist you had nothing to do with the little run that effectively smashed my operations on the coast, eh?"

Justin met his gaze calmly. "I'm surprised you ever thought I did. I thought we knew each other better than that."

"You must admit, your disappearance was extremely timely."

Justin shrugged. "I was lucky."

"So you say. In my business, I'm forced to face the fact that we make our own luck."

Justin remained silent.

"And the purpose of your trip now is...?"

"I told you. I'm taking Melanie to visit a former college classmate."

"Ah, yes. Your so-beautiful wife. Indeed, that does surprise me. You never used to let anyone get too close to you." He dropped his feet off the desk and leaned forward. "So what have you been doing with yourself during the past ten years?"

Justin chose his words with care. "When the operations fell apart I decided to head back north. I found a businessman who wanted to expand his operations to South America. I convinced him I knew the area and had contacts down here." He shrugged, keeping his eyes trained on his opponent. "So he hired me."

"You mean you've been down here for years, and this is the first time we've run into each other? I'm surprised."

"I haven't been working out of Colombia. Most of my time has been spent in Argentina."

"I see. Was there some particular reason you didn't come back here?"

"I wasn't sure who was left. I never knew whether you'd been taken on that raid or not. Most of my contacts were within our group. I heard three of them were killed. I didn't wait any longer to see who had survived."

Victor sighed. "I wish I could believe you, amigo. I really do. Unfortunately, too much hangs in the balance for me. If there is one chance in a thousand you are lying to me, I refuse to take the chance. I have too much to lose to allow you to leave here."

Justin continued to look Victor in the eyes, refusing to let him see the effect his words had on him. "You intend to keep us here?" His voice reflected only idle curiosity.

Victor laughed. "I like your style, man. I really do. Why would I keep you here? I have no use for you. Now your wife—she's another matter. I'm sure I would find her quite useful...in one way or another."

Justin recalled his last glimpse of Melanie, lying in bed, still shaken from the sudden interruption they had experienced. He didn't want to try to visualize what could happen to her if Victor made good his threats.

The question was, what was he going to do now? Victor enjoyed his position of power and was playing with him.

"You could always put me back to work for you," Justin replied lazily, his eyes watchful.

Victor's eyes narrowed slightly. "Why would I want to do that?"

"Because I was one of your best men, and you know it."

Victor nodded slowly. "I won't argue with you on that. But I don't need any more help."

Justin smiled slowly. "That's hard to believe on a place this size. You probably need all the help you can get, moving freight around, maintaining the equipment."

Victor's eyes narrowed. "You mean you'd work as a handyman around here?"

"It's better than staying locked up all day."

"You didn't seem to have trouble finding something to do when I found you this morning."

"I never figured you for the type who got his kicks from watching, Victor," Justin deliberately drawled. "Must be a sign of old age." His comment was a calculated move that could get him killed. It could also show Victor that he wasn't intimidated by him.

Victor stared at him for a moment in surprise, then threw his head back and laughed. "None of my women have complained yet, amigo." He shook his head. "But none of them are as beautiful as your wife. I wouldn't mind showing her that I have only improved with age."

Justin straightened in his chair. "Forget it. What is mine, I keep. I don't share."

Victor stood up, his arms stretched high above his head. "We'll see." He dropped his arms. "We need to eat. Come." He motioned to the door. "Afterward I'll find something to keep you busy. Perhaps your wife will thank me, eh?" He laughed again as they walked into the hallway.

Justin glanced up the stairs. "Let me get Melanie. I'm sure she's hungry, as well."

"You pamper her too much. No wonder North American women are so spoiled. They're too used to getting their own way."

"I don't see that feeding them is exactly spoiling them."

"But if you wait until they are good and hungry, you'd be surprised how much more willing they are to please you." Victor's wolfish grin made his meaning unmistakable.

Justin started up the stairway. "I'll see if she wants anything."

Victor called after him. "You do that. She may surprise you and tell you she wants a real man, not a servant waiting on her every moment. If so, tell her I'll be glad to oblige." His laugh followed Justin onto the balcony and into the room.

Justin closed the door behind him, finding the lock and making sure it was secure. He turned around and found Melanie standing in front of the window watching him, her eyes filled with apprehension.

"Is he going to take us to Villa Vicencias?"

"I wish it were that simple. No. He isn't going to take us anywhere."

Melanie walked over and sat down on the bed.

"I wished to hell I'd never brought you with me," Justin said, pacing across the floor. "If I'd left you at the village, you would have had some chance to get away."

"Are you saying I don't have a chance now?" she asked quietly.

"I don't know. The only reason he has left you alone so far is because he thinks we're married. Otherwise he'd have you in his bed right now."

She flinched at the harsh tone of his voice. "Then I'm glad you told him we're married."

He stopped his pacing and studied her. "Even after what almost happened this morning?"

"There's no reason to take the blame for that. We were both participants." She tried to smile. "At least it helped to convince Victor of our relationship."

"That's a point. But if I hadn't brought you with me, there would be no need to convince Victor of anything about you."

"It's too late to wish things were different. We need to decide what to do now."

"I know. Victor said he'd put me to work after breakfast. At least that will get me out of here and give me a chance to figure out a way to escape. Do you want to come downstairs to eat?"

"Not really. I'm afraid seeing Victor would take away whatever appetite I have."

"It's probably a good idea for you to stay out of his way as much as possible. I'll bring you something, if you don't mind staying up here all day."

"I don't mind. Did you notice the books?" She nodded toward a bookcase opposite the bed. "I'm surprised your friend would take the time to collect them."

"They aren't his. I think he commandeered this place from the original owner." He saw no need to mention what he believed had happened to the previous owner.

She smiled. "Then I'll wait for you here. I'm sure there's enough reading material to keep me entertained."

If he hadn't already recognized how he felt about her, Melanie's attitude would have forced Justin to face how much she meant to him. He had caught a glimpse of the fear in her smile, but her courage dominated. She was doing whatever was necessary to cope with their situation.

Knowing that touching her was not going to help him at the moment, he nevertheless walked over to her and took her hand, slowly drawing her to her feet and against him. She wrapped her arms around his waist and hugged him.

Justin placed a light kiss on each of her eyelids.

"I'll get you out of here safely. I promise you." The roughness in his voice did not detract from the sincerity.

"I know you will."

Unable to resist her soft lips, he leaned down and kissed her. Her mouth opened to his, and he felt the slight quiver she gave when his tongue increased their intimacy.

He abruptly stepped back from her, ruefully shaking his head. "My God, woman, what you do to me! I can't seem to keep my mind on anything else but you whenever I'm around you. That could get us killed, you know."

Melanie grinned. "Am I supposed to apologize?"

"Damned right!" He matched her grin. "No one should be as beautiful as you. There should be a law against it." Justin ran his hand through his hair, rearranging the already tousled waves that fell across his forehead. "I'll be back with some food for you as soon as I can." He turned away, unlocked the door and left.

Melanie sank onto the bed, thankful Justin hadn't discovered how his kiss had affected her. Her knees were obviously on a direct line with her heart and mouth because every time he kissed her, her heart tripled its normal beat and her knees gave out.

She glanced out the window again. While he had been gone she had watched several trucks pull in.

Several men had appeared and began unloading them, carrying boxes away from the house, down a trail that disappeared in the thick foliage of the jungle that surrounded the place.

Melanie wondered what they were unloading and where it was being taken. Not that it would do her much good to find out, but she was curious.

After Justin brought her a tray of food and cautioned her not to open the door to anyone but him, she ate, then found a book to read. Every so often she would glance out the window at the shouted commands and the sound of hurried feet. More trucks arrived during the day. She found the activity in the compound distracting and eventually put the book down and sat by the window, studying the activity.

She caught a glimpse of Victor and Justin. Justin was listening to Victor explain something, his arm pointing toward the path where the workers carried the boxes. Justin nodded, then they both took the path. Melanie watched until they disappeared.

If there were only something she could think of to do that would help. With so much activity going on outside, now would be a good chance to explore the house. Even if someone saw her she could explain that she was thirsty and looking for the kitchen.

Cautiously she opened the door and peered out. The coast was clear. Stepping out on the balcony, she peeked over the railing. There was no one in sight.

Should she explore upstairs first? That might be a little harder to explain. Gathering her courage, she made her way silently down the stairs. Over the next fifteen minutes Melanie wandered through the house. The home was beautiful—well laid out, comfortably furnished, reflecting nothing of Victor. She wondered how long he'd lived there.

Eventually she came across the kitchen where she found a middle-aged woman cutting up vegetables. Since the woman had her back to the door, Melanie stepped back into the hallway, wondering if she should ask for something to drink. Perhaps it would be better not to let the woman know she had left her room.

Returning to the entry hall, Melanie realized she had not yet gone into the room with the closed door. She wondered what it was. Listening closely she could hear nothing. She tried the handle and found that it turned easily and quietly. When she opened the door she discovered the room to be empty. With a sigh of relief she stepped inside, closing the door behind her.

At one time the room must have been used as a library or study, but most of the books had been removed from the shelves. The large ornate desk had been misused, its scarred surface a silent testimony to someone's lack of respect for fine wood.

One wall held more weapons than she had ever seen. Most of them she didn't recognize, although some of the pistols were similar to the one her brother had used to teach her target shooting.

She glanced over her shoulder. No one would miss it if she took one of the pistols. She didn't know if it would do her any good, but it might be worth the risk. She opened it to make sure it had bullets. It did—five of them. After rearranging the others so that no gap showed, Melanie held the pistol by her side and went over to the door.

After listening for any sounds she opened it and slipped out into the hallway.

She was halfway up the stairway when Victor and two of his men walked in the front door. He immediately saw her.

Melanie held the pistol between her palm and thigh, praying he wouldn't see it.

"Were you looking for me *señora*?" he asked with a dangerous smile.

"Uh, no, not really. I was thirsty and thought I'd see if I could get something to drink."

"Then why are you going up the stairs?"

"Well, uh, I heard someone coming. Justin told me not to leave the room, so—" she waved her other hand slightly, shrugging.

"So. You do not always obey your husband's instructions, I see." Victor laughed. "I'm glad to hear it. Particularly when it gives me a better chance to get to know you. Come down. Drake will be busy for several hours yet. That should give us plenty of time."

The other two men disappeared down the hallway, leaving her alone with him. The pistol seemed to grow larger in her hand, and she prayed he hadn't seen it, since she held it slightly behind her. Oh, what she wouldn't give for a concealing skirt with a pocket in it.

She shook her head. "I can't. I'll just go back to our room and wait for Justin."

Victor moved slowly toward her until he was at the bottom of the stairway. He smiled beguilingly. "Do not be afraid of me, little one. I would never harm such a pretty one as you. Come down and I will have Lupe make us something to drink. Okay?''

Melanie eased backward up to the next step, then the next. She was almost at the top of the stairway. "No. I'm sorry, but I can't." Her voice sounded polite but cool, and she was glad he couldn't hear the fear that clutched her when he had so suddenly appeared.

His smile widened. "Then perhaps I will join you upstairs. That is an even better idea. I am sure we will find ourselves much more comfortable."

One more step and she was on the balcony. She couldn't risk checking to see how far she was from their bedroom door. For some reason Melanie felt it crucial that she never take her eyes off Victor. She turned slightly so that her hand was concealed and walked along the balcony to the door. Should she close and lock it? No doubt he had a key. How long would it take him to find one? He'd had one earlier in the day.

Melanie searched for alternatives. Would she shoot him if he tried to attack her? Could she shoot him? She'd never shot anything in her life.

Victor took his time coming up the stairway. There was no doubt in her mind that he intended to follow her into the room, and Justin was too far away to hear her if she screamed.

Oh, Justin, I should have listened to you! The thought did her very little good at the moment.

Victor paused at the top of the steps. Melanie stood in the doorway, her hand hidden behind the facing.

She now held the pistol in her hand, her finger curled around the trigger.

A tremendous explosion suddenly shook the house, causing Melanie to almost lose her balance. For one wild moment she thought she might have already squeezed the trigger. Then she realized the noise had come from outside.

Victor was a step ahead of her. He'd already spun on his heel and raced down the steps, yelling orders. Melanie leaped inside her room and slammed the door, locking it. She glanced down at the pistol in her hand, wondering what to do with it. After stuffing it under one of the pillows on the bed she hurried to the window, trying to see what had happened.

Two trucks still stood in the compound. Men were running down the path where Justin and Victor had gone earlier in the day. Melanie felt a burning sensation in her chest and realized she had been holding her breath. She forced air out of her lungs, taking deep breaths and trying to stay calm.

All she could think about was Justin. Did the explosion have anything to do with him?

Black clouds of smoke rose in the air about half a mile from the house. She wondered what was over there. Despite her curiosity Melanie had no intention of leaving her room to find out. Her close call had been enough of a lesson.

Her heart seemed to jump into her throat when she heard the sound of gunshots. What was going on? And where was Justin?

Minutes marched by on leaden feet, and she slowly sank to the chair by the window, where she could watch the trail on which she hoped Justin would soon appear.

Voices raised in excitement reached her some time later and she leaned forward. Two men were carrying a third between them with no particular care. When they reached the compound they dropped him and she realized he was dead.

"Oh my God!" She stared at the motionless body, then forced herself to take note of his dark hair and clothes. Of course it wasn't Justin. She tried to swallow but something seemed to be stuck in her throat.

Others came hurrying along the path, talking and gesturing. Two of them carried another man. This time there was no mistaking him. It was Justin.

Five

Elise Trent woke up suddenly and found herself shaking. It had only been a nightmare, that's all. Only a nightmare. Ever since her sister Melanie had disappeared in Colombia she had been having the same type of dreams—where she was running through ever-expanding jungles, the path never changing. She would call for help but no one ever answered.

"What's the matter, love, can't you sleep?" Damon murmured from the darkness beside her. He was so much aware of her that he could sense when she was upset about something, even if he'd been asleep.

"I didn't mean to wake you," she whispered. "Go back to sleep."

He pulled her against him, nuzzling her neck and stroking her spine until she began to relax against his strong, muscled body.

"I'm scared, Damon. Really scared. It's been four days since you talked to Justin. Why hasn't he called? Now *both* of them have disappeared!"

"Hush, baby, don't let your imagination cause you more pain. Remember that Colombia has some primitive areas in it. There isn't a phone booth on every street corner like we have here. In fact there are damn few street corners." He kissed her softly on the lips. "I have complete confidence in Justin. No matter what might have caused Melanie not to show up at Maria Teresa's on schedule, Justin will be able to take care of it." His voice was low and soothing. "They're going to be all right. Maria Teresa said she would call the minute she heard from her, remember?"

Elise curled closer to his warm body and nodded.

"Who knows? Maybe Justin is using this opportunity to get better acquainted with your baby sister. You never can tell." She felt his grin against her cheek.

"You really think so?"

"Knowing Justin the way I do, probably the only danger Melanie has faced is to her virtue."

"Not Justin, Damon. He would never take advantage of her."

He sighed. "That's true. He's nothing like me in that respect."

She couldn't help but laugh at his satisfied tone of voice. "You aren't exactly a despoiler of virgins, you know."

"Maybe not. But from the time I got close enough to grab you, there was no chance you were going to ever get away from me."

"Big, tough man. If I hadn't gone to see you after your eye surgery, you would never have gotten in touch with me again."

"That's what you think. I was just giving you time to get used to the idea of us together."

"Oh, were you?"

"Umm-hmm." He kissed her again, this time with a slow, sensuous sureness that never failed to arouse her.

She pulled her mouth away from him slightly. "Do you really think they're safe?"

"As safe as Justin can possibly make it."

"Maybe he won't have as much control over everything as you think."

"I've placed my money on Justin for years, love. He's never let me down yet."

"I hate sitting here, waiting for the phone to ring."

"There isn't much else we can do."

"We could fly to Villa Vicencias."

"What good would that do?"

"I don't know. Somehow, we'd be closer to them. Maybe we could start some sort of search from there."

"Give it a few days, love. If we haven't heard anything by then, I'll make arrangements to fly down there."

"Oh, Damon. I love you so much. You understand what it feels like, don't you? Just waiting and waiting?"

"Of course I do. Justin is the brother I never had . . . Melanie the sister."

They lay there in silence for a few moments, Damon's hands slowly sliding over Elise's warm and responsive body.

"Do you realize what you're doing to me, touching me like that?" Elise finally muttered.

"Umm-hmm. I thought now would be a good time for one of your famous sleeping pills . . . they're guaranteed to take care of anything that ails you, I can testify to that."

Elise relaxed in his arms, praying that Damon's predictions concerning the safety of their loved ones were accurate.

Melanie bit down hard on her knuckles to keep from crying out while she watched the men carry Justin through the compound. They disappeared from view and she ran to the door, fumbling with the lock. She threw the door open and raced for the stairs. The men had come in from the rear entrance of the house and were just coming down the hallway. For a moment Melanie froze. She wasn't sure how she was going to react when she got a good look at him.

Victor was giving rapid orders, pointing to the stairs when he saw her standing at the top of them.

"Your husband is a lucky man, *señora*. Damned lucky. A barrel of gasoline got knocked over during the unloading and before anyone had sense enough to recognize what had happened, it exploded. Drake was closest and the explosion threw him across the hangar, knocking him out.''

He motioned for the men to carry Justin up the stairs. ''The clumsy idiot who spilled the gasoline won't be so stupid again, I assure you.''

The men carrying Justin reached her, and she spun around and ran to the bedroom. Jerking the covers back, she waited for them to bring him inside.

''Please be careful,'' she said as they jostled him through the doorway. They looked at her blankly. She shook her head. No one understood her but Victor, and the less she said to him the better.

She motioned to the bed, and they awkwardly carried him over to it and placed him there. She knelt beside the bed. He looked so pale except for the streaks of sweat and dirt that testified to the heavy labor he'd been doing. She checked his pulse. It seemed slow and steady. She suddenly wished for Elise and her medical knowledge.

Melanie went into the bathroom, emptied the bowl that held guest soap and filled it with warm water. She brought the bowl of water and a washcloth into the bedroom and sat them down beside the bed. Then she began to unbutton his shirt.

The shirt had been ripped, and when she pulled it off she could see where Justin had been hit by something along his side. It was scraped and bleeding, and he groaned when she shifted him to remove the shirt.

She began to bathe him gently, cleaning his face and neck. His eyes flickered open.

''Melanie?''

She could barely hear him. "I'm right here, Justin. Try to rest."

"What happened?"

"There was an explosion. Some gasoline exploded, and you were thrown by the blast."

He rolled his head on the pillow. "My head feels like it was stomped on by an elephant."

She chuckled. "I don't think they keep elephants around here."

"Where's Victor?"

"I don't know and I don't care, just so long as he doesn't come in here!"

Justin shifted restlessly on the bed. "Has he bothered you in here?"

Technically he hadn't for the simple reason she hadn't been in there at the time. Smiling at him reassuringly, she answered truthfully. "No."

He relaxed slightly. "At the moment I don't feel strong enough to put up much of a fight if he tried anything."

Melanie thought of the pistol hidden under the pillow. "I'm not worried." Although she might have qualms about using the weapon against Victor to save herself, she suddenly realized she would have no compunction in using it to protect Justin.

How interesting! Where had that fierce protective instinct sprung from? She glanced back down at Justin. He had closed his eyes, and she had the opportunity to study his face—the strong, masculine jawline and square chin, the heavy brows that almost met at the bridge of his nose, the slight irregularity of his nose that hinted at a break sometime or another.

She brushed his hair away from his face and smiled. For the first time she had an opportunity to look after him for a change.

By evening Justin appeared to feel much better. He had managed to shower and accompany her downstairs for dinner.

Victor was an expansive host, his smile flashing at Melanie repeatedly as he regaled them with stories in which he always appeared to be the hero of the moment.

Justin shifted uncomfortably in his chair. Every muscle and bone in his body seemed to ache, which didn't improve his disposition at all. Admittedly Melanie wasn't encouraging Victor, but his attitude toward her was definitely proprietory and growing more so by the hour.

"It's been a long day, Victor. I believe that Melanie and I will turn in now." He pushed his chair back and stood up.

Melanie immediately laid her napkin down and stood, as well.

"I can understand your need for rest, Drake, but I see no reason for you to deprive me of your wife's company so early in the evening."

Melanie saw Justin's hands clench at his sides. "I'm really tired myself. I don't mind going to bed this early."

Victor laughed. "I'm afraid your husband will be of little use to you tonight, Señora Drake. I, on the other hand, would be happy to oblige you."

Try as she might not to let his crude remarks affect her, Melanie could feel the hot color wash over her face. However, she forced herself to return Victor's stare calmly, her chin slightly lifted. "I love my husband, Señor Degas. I will stay with him."

Justin's gaze narrowed slightly, watching the interplay. If he hadn't known better he would have believed she was very happily married. Perhaps she'd missed her calling. With acting talent like that she shouldn't be wasting her time selling novelty gifts.

Victor nodded his head slowly. "I can wait."

Justin clenched his jaw, determined not to rise to the bait. He knew Victor was needling him, hoping to draw a reaction, pushing Justin to lose control.

Melanie walked out of the room ahead of Justin. They went up the stairs in silence, not speaking until the door was closed and locked behind them.

"We've got to get away from here!" Melanie exclaimed.

Justin's control slipped and he glared at her. "What the hell do you think I've been trying to do!"

The tense situation had made both their nerves raw.

She returned his glare with one of her own. "Trying to get yourself killed!"

"Hardly. It takes more than a scraped side and a headache to do me in."

He sat down on the side of the bed and wearily untied his boots. That reminded her of the pistol. She went over to the bed and drew it out.

"I found this while you were gone," she said quietly.

He glanced over his shoulder, and when he saw what she held he came to his feet. "Where'd you get that?"

"I found it downstairs."

"Downstairs! Do you mean to tell me you went downstairs today when I specifically told you to stay up here?" His voice began to rise.

Realizing that she had picked the wrong time to show him what her efforts at helping them had turned up, Melanie answered him in a low, soothing voice. "I'm not a child, Justin. I couldn't pass up the opportunity to find a possible way out of here."

"What the hell did you think I was doing out there?" He waved his hand. "Loading boxes for the exercise?"

"Were you able to find a possible weapon we could use?"

"Of course not. I wasn't looking for one. Believe it or not, Melanie, all I'm looking to do is to get away from here, not to kill somebody."

"I don't intend to kill anyone, either. But having a pistol gives us a little more of an advantage, doesn't it?"

"Do you think we're going to scare anybody around here with that when everyone is fully armed? One shot and a dozen men would come running. If you carry a gun you'd better damn well intend to use it.

Otherwise it's worthless...or worse. It can get you killed, because if you don't use it the other guy can take it away from you and use it on you."

"I hadn't looked at it that way."

"That's great. So you risked your neck to get the damned thing. What if Victor had caught you?"

"He didn't!" She certainly wasn't going to tell him how close he'd come.

Frustrated with her lack of understanding, he walked over to her, took her shoulders and lightly shook her. "Don't you understand that Victor intends to have you as soon as he can figure out how to get rid of me? If he could provoke me into fighting him, he'd use it as an excuse to kill me. Knowing Victor, he doesn't need much of an excuse."

She remembered the man who had died earlier in the day and shivered.

Justin felt the movement and swore under his breath. What the hell was he doing, taking out his fear and frustration on her? He pulled her to him and held her close, needing her warmth.

Nothing seemed all that frightening when Justin had his arms around her and she began to relax, her body fitting itself intimately to his. He leaned down and placed his lips on hers.

His touch started a tingling sensation within her that seemed to start at her toes and move throughout her body. She could feel the uneven beat of his heart beneath her fingertips as she pressed them against his chest.

The kiss seemed to sear her with its intensity, like molten lava cascading around her, holding her in place, pliant in his arms. His hands pressed her closer, ever closer to him until she felt as though she were a part of him.

He explored her mouth with an intensity of purpose that said more than words could express. She belonged to him, and he was making sure she understood that. No man would ever touch her—not as long as he was alive.

Justin's kiss had been intended as an apology and a comforting caress, but he soon forgot what had originally prompted the gesture. Melanie's response erased the past few hours from his memory.

His desire to protect Melanie from the jungle and from Victor became submerged in his desire to protect her from the emotions she evoked within him. He loved her, and he wanted her with a quiet desperation that had been steadily building inside of him during their enforced time together.

However, he needed to keep his head. He couldn't protect her from a pregnancy and he knew she would not be prepared for intimacy.

Justin forced himself to loosen his grip around her and reluctantly lifted his head. He made the mistake of opening his eyes—and saw her flushed cheeks and rosy mouth waiting for his kiss once more—and he was lost to the wonder of the moment.

"Oh, Melanie," he whispered, his words resembling a moan. Picking her up in his arms and carrying her the few feet to the bed, he carefully laid her down, then swiftly followed her to the comfortable surface.

As soon as Justin kissed her, Melanie experienced the same rush of feeling his lovemaking had evoked that morning. She no longer recognized her own reactions. Justin had introduced her to a new world of sensuous pleasure and thoughts of who she was, who he was and how their lives were linked together disintegrated in the heat of the night and his lovemaking.

For a moment Melanie knew she only cared about the fact that this was Justin and she loved and wanted him.

Melanie's response wiped every thought from Justin's head except one—she wanted him as much as he wanted her.

He reminded himself to be gentle with her, not to frighten her with his urgency. Instead he wanted to instill the moment with the specialness it deserved. His love for her was much more than a need for physical satisfaction. He wanted her to achieve the ultimate in pleasure, to know the joy of release and the soaring sensation true fulfillment can give.

Melanie discovered that she had already learned how to respond to Justin and had quickly grown accustomed to his touch. She found herself pressing closer to him, her hands outlining the heavy muscles in his back and shoulders. She was careful not to touch his injured side, although at the moment he seemed to be unconscious of it.

Her hands slipped underneath his shirt and explored the heavy mat of hair on his chest, loving the feel of him, wanting him to be closer to her so that she might experience the joy of his possession.

Justin began to undress her, caressing her as each item he removed revealed a new portion of her to him.

Pausing only to remove his clothes, Justin stretched out on the bed beside her once again. He gently stroked her bottom lip with his finger and reluctantly whispered, "Melanie, if you want me to stop, you'd better tell me. Right now!"

Her eyes slowly opened and she gazed at the tension in his face, reflected by his clenched jaw. She smiled. "Please don't stop," she said softly.

Her green eyes stared up at him beguilingly and he groaned. He didn't think a speeding locomotive could stop him at that point. He shifted slightly, adjusting his length and weight to accommodate her smaller frame. "I don't want to hurt you," he muttered, his mouth finding hers again.

When she could speak, she whispered, "You could never hurt me, Justin. Just love me...please love me."

Melanie felt the unfamiliar sensation of his possession and involuntarily tensed. He paused, his hands softly caressing her. "Try to relax, little one."

Her eyes slowly opened and she stared at the man above her, who filled her vision so completely, and knew that no one else would ever be able to fill that vision for her. Justin was more man than she had ever imagined existed. She wanted him desperately.

She arched her body, forcing his entry and for a short moment the pain shot through her. Then he was with her completely. The sensation was indescribable.

She belonged to him now. He would always be a part of her.

Justin began a slow rhythm, aware of her lack of knowledge, wanting so much to make the experience something wonderful for her. He recognized something he'd never felt before. Loving her made the act of possession a commingling of their spirits. The melting tenderness that flowed over him created a need to express his feelings with murmurs and caresses that, together with the steady rhythm of his lovemaking, brought her to the pinnacle of sensation.

Melanie gasped, her eyes flying open in amazement at what she was feeling.

"It's all right, love. It's all right. I want you to let go, just let go and soar," he whispered.

She clung to him tightly, the inner tension leaving her gradually as she seemed to float back into the room. Justin continued to hold her in his arms, kissing her face with a soft, gentle touch.

"Oh, Justin, I had no idea it could be like that."

"Neither did I," he admitted.

She stroked her hand languidly through his hair. "You mean you enjoyed it, too?" she asked in a lazy voice.

"I am *still* enjoying it," he said with a grin, as he slowly began their intimate rocking once more.

Her eyes opened wide. "You mean there's more?"

"A true gentleman always allows his lady to go first," he pointed out just before his lips claimed hers once again.

Melanie lost track of time and space and gave herself up to his expert tutoring. He taught her about her own sensuality as well as his. When he gave a final lunge and collapsed, she couldn't help but wonder if all men made love the same. If so, she wondered how women could bear to let them leave home to go to work. She'd want to keep him tied to the bed!

Melanie drifted off into sleep after Justin shifted to his uninjured side, bringing her to lie against him. Eventually Justin drifted off while trying to figure out how to get her away from there before Victor made good his threats.

Sometime later Justin woke up suddenly, then listened, trying to decide what had brought him out of a sound sleep. He heard nothing.

It was the lack of noise—the total silence—that had stirred him into wakefulness. Where were the night noises of the jungle that surrounded them? He listened, trying to pick up some sound, some call of an animal or night bird.

The moon was high in the sky, and the bars covering the window striped the bed in shadow. He glanced down at Melanie lying so close beside him.

For the first time in days he thought of Damon and Elise worrying about them, wondering why he hadn't gotten back in touch with them. It was better that Elise not know just how dangerous the situation was for her baby sister. She wouldn't rest any easier knowing that her sister had been posing as his wife for several days now.

And what if Elise knew you had made love to her? he asked himself. He had had no intention of making love to Melanie until they were safe from this place. He'd known that it was only a matter of time, but this wasn't the time, dammit, nor the place, and he was disgusted with himself.

She was so responsive in his arms—so warm and loving. He could have spent the entire night loving her. Even the thought of their lovemaking aroused him, and he shifted restlessly, giving a low moan.

The slight sound awakened Melanie and she blinked, trying to figure out where she was. The moonlight had caused strange shapes and shadows in the room. She realized the noise she had heard had come from Justin, and she moved her head slightly where it lay on his shoulder and glanced up at him.

Although he had made no other sound, she could see the light reflecting off his eyes. He was awake.

"Are you in pain?" she whispered.

His arm tightened around her convulsively. "No," he murmured softly.

"What's wrong?"

He didn't want to tell her. He was behaving like some sex-starved teenager rather than a thirty-seven-year-old man.

She moved her hand that had been resting on his chest, rubbing it across the furry mat in a lazy caress.

"Nothing," he said, in a strangled voice.

"Are you sorry you made love to me?"

"No."

"Neither am I. I thought it was wonderful," she said dreamily. "And so romantic. The way you picked me up and carried me to the bed. The way you took my clothes off so slowly, touching me everywhere."

"Uh, yeah, well, you'd better get some more rest."

"I know. You need your sleep, too. Am I too heavy on your arm?" Her hand brushed down across his stomach, abdomen, and—

He grabbed for her hand but he was too late. She had already discovered his arousal that had been further stoked by her caresses. Her fingers touched the smooth surface in discovery, and he slowly let his hand fall back to his side.

He let out a shuddering breath. If her actions were anything to judge by, she seemed to be enjoying his state.

"Show me how to make love to you," she whispered.

"You're doing a fantastic job of it, love. You don't need any more instruction."

"You mean like this?"

He nodded, a moan escaping him.

"And this?"

"Oh, God, yes, Melanie."

"I love the feel of your body. The skin is so smooth, but just underneath the skin the muscle is so taut. I can feel it ripple wherever I touch you."

He could take no more. He pulled her over on top of him and, raising his head slightly, brushed his lips against the tips of her breasts. She caught her breath.

"Oh," she murmured breathlessly.

"Did I hurt you?"

"Oh, no."

His tongue slowly stroked her breast until she was unable to stay still. Her provocative movements enabled him to slip deep inside of her. She gasped.

"Is that uncomfortable?" he asked.

She shook her head and smiled. His heart turned over. Her braid had come undone and her hair fell around them, creating a veil effect over them. The moon cast its light over her, gilding her with an aura of silver.

"Oh, Melanie..."

"What is it?"

"I love you so much."

"I'm so glad. I love you, too."

The words were soft and spoken in rhythm to their bodies' movements. Melanie had thought that nothing could ever compare to the first time he had made love to her, but now Justin showed her variations on the love theme that entranced her with their subtleties.

Her body became an instrument of pleasure, and Justin knew what strings to touch to bring her alive. He kissed and caressed her until she became mindless. She couldn't contain the sensations as her body seemed to lift her up, higher and higher until she felt as though she were one with the universe, experiencing the true meaning of life and love and the joy of sharing.

When Justin gave one final lunge she felt inseparable from him, as though they had both tumbled off the edge of the earth, hurtling through space in a gentle rocking movement, as though the bed still vibrated from their movements of love. Not only the bed, but the room, the house, the earth—all seemed to rock in harmony to their fantastic joining.

She collapsed in his arms, limp and totally unable to move. But it seemed as though the bed, the room, the house—even the earth—still trembled.

Then Justin rolled over and abruptly sat up.

"My God! I should have recognized the signs!" He leaped out of bed. "It's an earthquake!"

Six

"Get your clothes on! Quick! We've got to get out of here."

Justin's jarring move and incisive voice pierced through the fog of sensual satiation that had totally enveloped Melanie, suddenly dumping her out of her warm emotional clouds into harsh reality. All that she had really caught was that he wanted her to get her clothes on and get up.

She had never imagined that her first night of love-making would end in this manner. Not that she had expected a pledge of undying devotion and a demand for her hand in marriage—she wasn't that much of a romantic, but somehow Melanie had assumed she would at least be able to spend what was left of the night peacefully sleeping.

Justin heard a tremendous crash somewhere in the house and began to curse. He finished lacing up his boots, found his backpack and turned back to Melanie.

She stood beside the bed like a lost child, uncertain what to do next. Her jeans and shirt were in place—he thanked God for that—but she gazed around the room, bewilderment plain on her face. "Where are my shoes?" she wondered out loud.

Justin found them—one by his side of the bed, the other by the chair—and took them to her. Neither one of them had particularly cared what happened to her shoes earlier.

Plaster fell from the ceiling and the room began to sway alarmingly. A large crack appeared in the outside wall, the noise becoming deafening around them.

Justin picked up Melanie and sprinted across the floor, which swayed and undulated beneath his feet. Just as he threw open the door the roof caved in behind them.

Melanie screamed. It was her worst nightmare come true. Where could they go to be safe? The terrifying noise of beams and plaster crashing down surrounded them. Keeping as close to the wall as possible, Justin followed the balcony to the stairway, only to find a gaping hole where the stairs had been.

They were trapped. While Justin stood there with Melanie in his arms he felt the balcony on which they stood give way.

* * *

The phone by Damon's elbow rang and he absent-mindedly answered, his mind on the contract before him.

"Damon Trent."

"Damon!" Elise was never so glad to hear any-one's voice in her life. "Oh, Damon!" She could scarcely talk.

"Elise! What's the matter? Have you heard from Melanie?"

"No. Oh, God, Damon! There's been an earth-quake in Colombia!"

"An earthquake? When?"

"A special news bulletin just came in over the ra-dio. I turned on the television but the news is sketchy. They say it was south of Bogotá, less than a hundred miles from Villa Vicencias. Oh, Damon. What are we going to do?"

"You stay right where you are, darling. I'll be home as soon as I can get there."

Elise hung up the phone and stared at the wall. Would she ever see Melanie again?

Five-year-old Eric walked into the room. "What's wrong, Mom?"

She did her best to get a grip on her emotions. There was no reason to upset Eric or Brenda. "I'm just worried about your Aunt Melanie, honey."

Eric sat down beside her and took her hand. He looked so much like Damon at the moment—with his earnest little frown—that she almost burst into tears.

"She's all right, Mom, don't worry. Remember what Daddy said. Uncle Justin is taking care of her."

"I know. I guess I just forgot." She tried to think of something else, anything else but the devastation an earthquake could do. She could still remember the pictures of the destruction caused by earthquakes in Mexico City. She ran her hand through Eric's thick, black hair. "What's Brenda doing?"

"Playing dress-up."

"Playing dress-up? What's she wearing?"

"Your lipstick and earrings and stuff like that."

"Oh, Lord, how did she find all of that?" Elise leaped from the sofa and ran down the hallway, hoping to be able to rescue some of her cosmetics.

When Damon arrived home shortly thereafter, he heard Elise's voice coming from their bedroom. He paused in the doorway, taking in the scene before him.

Elise glanced up at him. For the past few minutes she had actually forgotten he was coming home.

Brenda had thoroughly enjoyed herself. Although not quite three she fully understood the wonders of self-improvement. She had liberally dusted her mother's face powder all over her black curls so that she now had beige curls. Lipstick covered her mouth, as well as her cheeks and eyebrows.

Several bracelets slid up and down on her chubby arms as she waved her hands in the air. "Daddy's home!"

"Don't tell me," Damon drawled. "Let me guess. The circus is in town, and Brenda has decided to join their tour."

Elise gave up trying to clean the makeup off her daughter's face and turned to him. "Oh, Damon." Nothing seemed quite so bad whenever he was there. She put her arms around him and clung.

He patted her back while still inspecting their daughter. "I don't believe that's really your shade of red, darlin'," he said to Brenda. "It's too harsh."

Brenda giggled. "Pretty girl, Daddy."

"You certainly are. But I don't think your mother needed this right at the moment."

Elise pulled away, wiping the tears before she turned around to face her daughter again. "I'm going to have to use cleansing cream, then I've got to shampoo your hair. You might as well learn what it takes to keep yourself beautiful, my dear." She swooped her up and took her into the bathroom, turning on the water full force.

Damon stepped into the room to watch. "I caught some of the news on the way home. It may not be as bad as they first feared. The quake seemed to limit itself to a small area, so there's a good chance Justin and Melanie won't even be affected by it."

"If we only knew where they were!"

"Yes, I've been thinking about that, and I believe you're right. If your mother won't mind watching Eric and Brenda, we'll fly down there and see what we can do to find them."

Elise looked up from bathing her squirming daughter. "Thank you, darling."

He smiled. "It wouldn't hurt you to have a little vacation away from these two, anyway."

Elise nodded, ducking her head to hide the tears that threatened to overflow again.

Justin groaned, opening his eyes. He was staring up at blue sky and bright sunlight. He tried to sit up and pain shot through him. Plaster and debris littered his body. He was bruised and bleeding and his clothes hung in shredded tatters around him.

That's when he remembered. He had been holding Melanie in his arms at the top of the missing staircase when the balcony had given way.

"Melanie!"

Most of the roof of the house was gone. Only a few walls were left standing. Nothing but rubble remained of the area of the house where the bedrooms had been located.

He started throwing boards and plaster off and stood up, his heart racing. Where was she? He had been holding her, he would never have let her go. She had to be nearby.

She was. She lay a short distance away. A ceiling beam lay between them so that he hadn't seen her until he stood up. He crawled over the beam and knelt by her side. There was a lump on the side of her head and her arm was scraped and bleeding, but she was breathing. Thank God she was breathing!

He came to his feet, looking around what was left of the entryway. Where was everybody? The place appeared deserted—or abandoned. He picked her up and carried her to the front of the house, stepping over what had once been a wall. The door still stood closed and locked.

He wondered if the original owner would feel that justice had been served. He also wondered if Victor had managed to survive. If he had been in his bedroom upstairs, he probably hadn't stood a chance. In fact, Justin was amazed that he and Melanie had managed to live through it.

He stretched her out under the shade at the edge of the clearing and went back to find whatever he could—water, food, survivors. He found the water, his backpack, and enough food to keep them for a couple of days.

There were no other survivors.

By the time he returned to her side, Melanie's eyes were open. She had seen him moving around the wrecked remains of the large home and dreamily waited for him to join her.

"So you finally decided to wake up, did you?" he asked with a grin. He handed her his canteen of water. "I thought you might plan to sleep all day." He bathed her forehead, checking the bump on her head. Some of the color had returned to her face but her pulse was rapid.

"You know, Justin, I've been thinking," she said, her face solemn.

His eyes met hers. "About what?"

"About us."

He smiled. "A very serious subject, I'll admit. What about us?"

"Do you think we should tone down our lovemaking a little? Just look what we did to this poor house." Her head turned slightly, and her gaze followed the jagged line of one of the half walls that remained.

"I don't know how to break the news to you, love, but we had nothing to do with this. Mother Nature caused it without any assistance from us." He gathered her up in his arms and held her close. She had survived the worst of it. *Please, God, don't let anything be seriously wrong with her now.*

"Oh, that's a relief," she murmured, closing her eyes.

He wondered if she was suffering from a concussion. She was making sense—sort of—but didn't seem to have fully recognized what happened.

"Do you remember the earthquake?"

She smiled, a beautiful, dreamy smile. "Oh, yes. Wasn't it wonderful?"

"Not particularly. Do you remember the ceiling almost crashing in on us?"

She thought for a moment. "No. But now I understand what the words to that song meant. I definitely felt the earth move under my feet."

"I'd love to take the credit for that sensation, but I'm afraid it wasn't me."

"Oh, well. I'm sure I'll enjoy your lovemaking just as much without all of this." She waved her hand.

"I think you need to rest," he said, becoming more concerned than ever. He pulled a jacket from his backpack and folded it under her head. "Why don't you relax while I look for some transportation. No one is around to stop us from borrowing whatever isn't damaged.''

He realized she missed the implication of that remark as she docilely lay back down and closed her eyes. And maybe it was just as well. What he had found in the wreckage wasn't a pretty sight, and he thanked God that he and Melanie hadn't ended up buried in the rubble as well.

Justin found a Jeep that appeared to be intact. He took the time to go out to the airstrip, where he'd been working the day before, hoping to find more provisions. The destruction there hadn't been quite so severe. He filled two cans full of gasoline and carried them back, filling the Jeep's tank with one and the storage tank at the rear of the Jeep with the other.

When he maneuvered the Jeep to where he had left Melanie, he found her asleep. He wasn't sure that was a good sign. He was very much afraid she had a concussion, but even if she did, there wasn't a hell of a lot he could do for her, except try to get her to a doctor.

He laid her in the back seat, then crawled behind the steering wheel and started the engine. The sooner he could find civilization, the better he'd feel.

After following the winding road for several hours, Justin was relieved to come across a village that was even larger than the one where he'd first found Melanie. However, from the look of things the earthquake had done some serious damage here, as well.

They had a small hospital but it was overflowing and the doctor was unable to find a place for Melanie. He did check her over carefully and confirmed the concussion, but said that a few days' rest would be all she needed.

Justin discovered that they wouldn't be able to go any farther anyway—the quake had destroyed the bridge that spanned the river south of the village.

They were less than a half day's drive to Villa Vicencias, but there was no way to get them there. The phone system in the village had been damaged by the quake. The villagers hoped it would be working before too much longer.

In the meantime, a room was made available for the tall American and his beautiful wife. Justin went to sleep that night with Melanie safe asleep in his arms, praying that there would be no more adventures or excitement for either of them for years to come.

Melanie woke up slowly the next morning and decided she must have the flu. Every muscle in her body ached, and her head felt as if it was trying to launch itself from her shoulders.

She was lying on her side, and she idly noted Justin's arm was draped possessively around her waist. She smiled. Justin had made love to her and what a wonderful experience that had been. But maybe it had been to much for her, and now her body was protesting.

Looking closer, she noticed a nasty bruise from his wrist to his elbow and wondered how he could have done that. Probably when the gasoline exploded. She decided to slip out of bed without awakening him and soak in the tub. Maybe that would help.

She managed to slide out from under his arm without disturbing him and stood up. The room spun dizzily around her. She sat down on the side of the bed for a moment and looked around. They were no longer in Victor's home. The room they shared was smaller. The wood floor was bare except for a woven grass mat by the bed. A mirror hung on a nearby wall, and she forced herself to walk over and peer into it.

One side of her face was swollen, and she had a multicolored bruise on her forehead. She turned around and looked at Justin. There were deep lines running from his nose to his mouth. The area below his closed eyes was shadowed as though he hadn't slept in days.

Melanie tried to remember her dreams. They were all mixed up with their lovemaking and the room shaking. She shook her head slightly, causing the throbbing to increase. Something had happened but she wasn't sure what. She was wearing her gown, but she didn't remember undressing the night before.

Looking around the small room, she noticed a door and when she opened it, found the bathroom. It certainly wasn't modern, but the tub was deep and when she tried the water, she was delighted to find it hot.

Melanie filled the tub and crawled in, enjoying the warmth of the water and the soothing sensation to all of her muscles. She closed her eyes and rested her head on the back of the tub.

She wasn't sure what had happened, but it appeared they had gotten away from Victor. Vague images danced in her head of crashing walls and trembling floors but she wasn't sure how much of it she had dreamed. Melanie rubbed her forehead. The knot on her head was definitely real, and the fact that her brain seemed to be packed away in cotton made thinking difficult.

If they had escaped from Victor, then there was no reason that they shouldn't reach Villa Vicencias soon. Melanie allowed her mind to drift back over the happenings of the past few days and she smiled. Despite the danger she would not have missed the chance to spend time with Justin for anything.

She knew that in the ordinary course of events she never would have experienced the wonder of Justin's lovemaking. If he hadn't been sent to find her, Justin never would have come willingly into her life.

As much as she loved him, she recognized there was no room in Justin's life for her. She believed him when he told her he loved her, but it wasn't the love on which a marriage was built. Justin was a loner and content with his life-style. His chivalrous rescue of her didn't change the basic nature of the man.

Melanie knew that sooner or later Justin would bring up their relationship. They could not ignore much longer the fact that he was in business and a close personal friend with her brother-in-law. However, she couldn't allow that relationship to influence what was happening between the two of them.

Somehow she would have to convince Justin, if he should bring up the subject, that she didn't expect him to marry her. No marriage could succeed that was based on an obligation by either party. Hopefully she could avoid the issue until they arrived at Villa Vicencias.

She could only try.

The water had begun to cool when the bathroom door swung open, and Justin leaned against the doorjamb.

"Good morning."

Melanie glanced up, and a sharp pain of loss shot through her at the sight of him. At the moment she wasn't sure how she would manage to get through the rest of her life without his presence. She only knew she had to try.

Forcing herself to become objective, she noticed he wore his jeans, which looked considerably worse for wear. His chest was bare and several livid bruises discolored the area.

"You look terrible," she finally commented after her silent survey.

He grinned. "Thank you. I was going to say how much better you look this morning."

She touched her forehead. "You mean this?"

"Everything. Your color is much improved. How do you feel?"

"Other than being sore and having a headache, I'm okay. Where are we?"

"Just a few hours away from Villa Vicencias."

Her eyes widened. "That's wonderful. Then we should be there by noon."

"I'm afraid not. Not only is the bridge gone but there was considerable damage to the road. I had a hell of a time getting this far yesterday. We're going to have to walk, I'm afraid, and I don't think you're in any condition to do that just yet."

She thought about it for a moment. "Well, maybe another day of rest would do it."

"Possibly."

"Is there any way we can call Maria Teresa and tell her where we are?"

"The phones are out, which isn't surprising."

"Oh." She thought about her family back home. "I bet Mom and Elise are really worried by now."

"I'm sure they are, particularly after the earthquake."

She sat up in the tub gingerly. "You mean there really was an earthquake?"

"You don't remember?"

She shook her head slowly, a frown of concentration creasing her brow.

He started to laugh.

"What's so funny?"

"I'll tell you some other time. Do you remember Victor's house being destroyed?"

"Vaguely. I remember bits and pieces of what seemed to be a nightmare. The stairway being gone...the ceiling falling in."

"That happened, although you're right. It seemed like a nightmare."

"Is that how we got away from Victor?"

"Yes. No one objected when I borrowed his Jeep."

She smiled. "Well, I'm glad we were able to get away from him, but an earthquake was a little drastic, don't you think?"

"Believe me, I didn't order one. How much longer are you going to be?"

"Oh, I'm through." She stood up and held out her hand for him to help her out of the old-fashioned tub.

The water had beaded on her skin and droplets made tantalizing trails across her firm, high breasts. One ran between them, sliding ever downward until it disappeared in the curls where her thighs met.

He took her hand and helped her out of the tub, then lifted a towel off the rack and began to blot her body. Her hair was already falling loose from the pins she had placed in it, the silky strands snaking down. One curled around his wrist.

She noticed her hair and sighed. "I've got to wash it, but I thought I would bathe first." She glanced up at Justin. His eyes had turned a deep blue and seemed to burn her with their message.

She went up on tiptoe and curled her arms around his neck, determined to enjoy whatever time together they had left. "Would you like me to scrub your back for you this morning?"

Her warm breasts pressed against his bare chest was more than he could resist. His arms came around her like steel bands and his mouth found hers. "Oh, Melanie, you feel so good," he managed to mutter.

"So do you," she murmured.

His hands settled possessively at her waist while his mouth leisurely explored hers. She felt so perfect in his arms as though she had been formed to fit his specifications.

He lifted her, his arms sliding behind her shoulders and knees, and carried her into the other room. When he lowered her to the bed her hands dropped from his shoulders to the front of his jeans. Yes, she had changed a great deal in the time they had been together.

Her participation in their lovemaking was equal to his and time no longer mattered to either of them. They became lost in the joy of sharing everything they were with each other.

Melanie discovered how much she benefited from pleasing Justin. His responses were immediate and profound, and when they reached their peak of pleasure she felt securely wrapped in his love.

Drowsily she turned her head to where his head rested next to hers on the pillow and kissed his jaw. "Thank you."

"For what?" he mumbled, raising his head slightly.

"For teaching me how to make love. You're very good at it."

"How would you know?"

"I just know."

"Well, for your information, young lady, I'm not going to give you the opportunity to do any comparison shopping."

"What do you mean?"

"That as soon as we reach civilization, we're getting married."

She edged away from him slightly. Melanie wasn't ready for that particular discussion, not right at the moment, not when the joy of being in his arms was still such a part of her. "What are you talking about?" she asked, hoping to gain a little more time in which to think about how she was going to tell him that she wasn't going to marry him.

He shifted on the bed slightly so that he could raise up on his elbow. "I'm talking about the fact that I want to marry you."

She shook her head a little sadly. "No, you don't."

He stared at her in surprise. "I don't?"

"No. But I understand why you offered. After all, I am Elise's baby sister and you are Damon's best friend. It could be rather awkward if they were to find out how we have spent this week."

"That is not why I want to marry you."

"You don't have to pretend, Justin. If you have never married before now, it's because you don't want to be married. It's really very simple," she explained in a patient voice.

"But, dammit, I do want to be married now. To you."

"You needn't raise your voice, I can hear you."

He rolled onto his back and stared at the ceiling. "I don't believe this. I have never asked a woman to marry me in my entire life and when I do, she turns me down."

"Don't take it so personally."

"Of course I'm going to take it personally. How the hell else should I take it?" He stared at her suspiciously. "Didn't you tell me you loved me?"

"Yes."

"Were you lying?"

"Of course not."

"Then why won't you marry me?"

"I've already told you, because you don't want to be married. You are living the life you want to live, don't you understand? If you hadn't come to Colombia looking for me, you wouldn't even be thinking about getting married."

"That may be true, but—"

"So let's just forget about what has happened between us since you arrived."

"You mean forget about—" he waved his hand to her lying unclothed next to him and their still-intimate position "—all of this?"

"Don't pretend that you have never spent similar times with other women because I won't accept that from you. You're too honest."

"I never said I had never been to bed with another woman, but I damn well know for sure I'm the first man *you've* made love to."

"Oh, so that's it. Well, you need feel no guilt over that. You certainly didn't force me. If you will recall, you received my full cooperation."

Justin sat up and swung his feet to the floor. "I'm going to get cleaned up, dressed and go find something to eat. After we've eaten we will continue this discussion."

Melanie nodded. "I'm hungry, too. But there's no reason to continue this conversation."

"That's what you think!" he muttered, stalking to the bathroom and firmly closing the door.

Melanie grabbed her brush and vigorously brushed her hair, then absently braided it. Well, she had done it. He had done the proper thing and proposed. She had done the proper thing and politely declined. She only wished it didn't hurt so much to do the proper thing. He really was going to play the rescuing white knight to the hilt.

She tried not to think about what it would be like to be married to him and to be Mrs. Justin Drake—living in Buenos Aires or wherever else he might live. Melanie sighed. She wasn't a child. And she wasn't going to confuse what they had shared with some romantic tale. She loved Justin and always would, but she wasn't going to allow that love to become a shackle around him.

No doubt the pretense during these past several days had given him the idea that he should offer. Fine. He had offered. Now his conscience should be clear.

She just didn't understand why he was so upset about her answer. Perhaps it was just as well she never intended to marry. She didn't think she would be able to understand the male mind if she lived to be a hundred.

Seven

Justin forced himself to calm down and think logically. All right, so he hadn't handled the scene well. But her attitude toward marriage had come as a complete surprise to him.

He should have thought it through first, he decided, scrubbing his body vigorously under the hot spray of water. Melanie had already made it clear she didn't want to be overprotected. He could understand that.

Perhaps she thought he was too old for her and didn't want to hurt his feelings by pointing that out. Was twelve years such a gap? It was hard to say. He was impressed with her maturity but then she was used to being around older people.

Surely she didn't see him as some sort of uncle figure. No way. Her loving response to him was certainly not familial.

Maybe she wanted to be courted. That made more sense. Here they had been thrown together into an intimate situation that had inevitably led to their lovemaking. But she didn't want their relationship to be taken for granted. Understandable. Of course he would have to wait until he got her back to Villa Vicencias. Once he did that he would— Oh hell! He would have to get back to Buenos Aires immediately to see if he could salvage anything of the deal with Jorge Villanueva.

Well, then, after that maybe he could fly to the States and talk to her about— About what? Leaving her family and friends, her business, to marry him?

Use your head. She never had any intention of marrying you. Just because you've discovered you can't live without her doesn't mean the feeling is mutual.

He turned off the water and grabbed a towel. His skin tingled from the rough usage he made of the innocent cloth. He couldn't think of one good reason why she should want to marry him.

When he walked back into the room, she was gone. The bed had been made up and their clothes laid out on top of it. After what they had been through recently, the choice was meager. At least these were cleaner than what they had recently had on.

He dressed in minutes, combed his hair and stepped outside into the hall of the small hotel. She was nowhere in sight.

Didn't she have any better sense than to wander away after all they had been through? That woman could dredge up more emotion in him quicker than anyone he had ever known. Damn her, anyway.

As soon as he stepped out into the sunshine he saw her. She sat on a long bench just outside the hotel door, holding a little boy that looked to be about four. It was obvious he had been crying.

She glanced up and saw him with relief. "Oh, Justin. Can you understand what he's saying? I found him sitting here crying. And just look at his foot. Something must have smashed it. It's so swollen."

Justin knelt down beside him, taking the small, grimy hand, and began to talk softly to him in Spanish. He found out that his name was Miguel and that he didn't know where he lived or where his mother was and that he was hungry.

Justin looked up and down the street in front of the hotel. There were many people moving back and forth, but no one seemed to be looking for a little boy. The ravages of the earthquake were obvious. There were many injured, others helping them. Some carried belongings as though they were not sure where to go.

"We'll take him to breakfast with us, then go to the hospital and have the doctor check him. Maybe someone has been looking for him over there."

He scooped Miguel up in his arms, and they went inside to eat.

Melanie didn't remember having seen the doctor nor the hospital the day before, so was shocked when they arrived to see how overcrowded they were.

The doctor explained that many had been brought in from outlying areas, but that luckily the damage to their town had been minimal. After checking Miguel's foot he discovered it was not broken but badly bruised. A woman who had brought in someone with an injury recognized Miguel and called out to him.

His face lit up and he hobbled over to her, throwing his arms around her. From what Justin could gather, the woman was his mother's sister, and she agreed to watch over him until either his mother appeared or she could take him back home.

"It looks as though you could use some help," Melanie said to the doctor.

His gray head nodded. "Yes. I have been very shorthanded. Our place here wasn't built to handle such a major disaster."

"Few places are. I would like to stay and help, if I could." She glanced at Justin. "Is that all right with you?"

"Whatever you want to do. I'm going to see if I can find a way to get us across the river. I know you're as anxious to get to Villa Vicencias as I am." His level gaze met hers, and her heart sank. He had never mentioned his proposal again, although she had waited all through breakfast for him to bring it up.

Obviously he felt he had made the offer, but wasn't going to push it, which was fine with her. Justin was extremely hard to resist. She loved him even more for thinking of her before himself. But she wasn't willing to accept that sacrifice from him.

Melanie spent the entire day at the hospital. By evening she was exhausted. Whether due to the recent strain and stress or the heavy work she had done that day, she discovered that there would be no reason to fear pregnancy from her recent exposure to Justin's virile charms.

The knowledge seemed to make an ending to what they had shared. She had given no thought to the possibilities of a pregnancy, which wasn't surprising. She had never had to concern herself before. So much had happened so quickly that the time she'd spent with Justin seemed more like a dream.

The reality was that there would be no aftereffects, no reason to prolong their relationship. They would go back to their own lives and forget what had happened in Colombia.

Justin went by the hospital looking for Melanie and was told she had left a short time before. He had spent the day talking with people, trying to find transportation into Villa Vicencias. There were no boats large enough to ferry the Jeep across and he finally resigned himself to another long hike, but at least it would be their last one.

He found Melanie curled up on their bed, asleep. Her face was flushed and she looked as though she had been crying. He sat down beside her and her eyes opened.

"Is anything wrong?" he asked.

"Not really. Nothing I don't go through every month."

He thought about that for a moment. "I see. I'm sure that's a relief to you."

"Of course. I wouldn't want you thinking I'd tried to trap you into anything."

He brushed her hair behind her ear and slowly stroked her back. "I would never think that, Melanie."

She smiled. "I'm glad. I hope you'll think kindly of me whenever you happen to remember me."

"You needn't worry about my ever forgetting you."

"I've been trying to decide how much I want to tell my family about what happened. If they knew about Victor and the danger we were in, I think they would just worry more than usual, don't you?"

"No doubt," he remarked dryly.

"So when we call them, let's just say you found me and it took us this long to find transportation."

"If that's what you want."

"I just don't want them worrying about me."

"I know. You love them very much, don't you?"

Her face lit up. "Oh, yes. And Eric and Brenda make the family complete."

"At least until you have some of your own."

She shook her head. "I don't intend to have children."

"But that's ridiculous. You gravitate to children and they to you. You'd make a marvelous mother."

She shook her head again, afraid to say anything for fear of crying.

"Well," he said, coming to his feet. "We certainly don't have to decide about your family tonight. Do you feel like going for something to eat?"

"I don't think so. I think I'll change into my gown and go to bed for the night so I'll be ready for our hike tomorrow."

"Do you think you're going to feel up to it?"

"Oh, I'll be fine by morning. You'll see."

"I'll bring you something to eat. How's that?"

"If it isn't too much bother."

"You're not a bother to me at all, Melanie. Not at all." He leaned over and kissed her cheek.

When the door closed behind her, tears slid down her cheeks once more. *I will get over him, I will get over him,* she chanted over and over softly.

When Justin returned to the room it was dark. He snapped on the bathroom light so he could see where to walk without awakening Melanie. Sometime during the day she had managed to get all of their clothes washed and the room smelled of freshly laundered clothes. The bathroom held the slight scent of her cologne and powder, and Justin recognized that he would never smell that scent again without thinking of her.

He hastily showered, hurrying so he wouldn't wake her. He found a neat stack of his undershirts and shorts and put on a pair of his briefs to sleep in. After turning out the light he padded softly over to the bed and eased into its narrow confines with her.

Only then did it hit him that there was no reason for them to be sharing a bed. There was no longer any danger, no reason to pretend they were married. And he knew that he could not sleep next to her without wanting to make love to her. The memories were too vivid and much better than his imagination.

But it was too late tonight to go ask for another room. Besides, she might wake up and wonder what happened to him. If everything worked out as planned, they would get a boat ride across the river in the morning and spend the next day hiking to Villa Vicencias. They might even be able to find a ride part of the way.

Although she didn't wake up, Melanie seemed to know he was there because she turned over, curling up beside him, her head on his chest. She smelled so sweet. Her hair felt like silk against his face. He would have one last night with her in his arms. The memories would have to last a lifetime.

A sharp rap on the door the next morning aroused Justin, and without thought he muttered, "Come in."

The last person he expected to see standing in the doorway was Damon Trent.

Damon froze for a moment, then stepped inside the room and slowly closed the door behind him. Leaning against it, he took in the intimate scene before him without expression. "Well, I can see there was no reason for us to worry about either one of you," he said in a low tone. "I can also see why you weren't in any hurry to get to Villa Vicencias."

Justin tried to sit up, but Melanie was still asleep on his arm, her back to the door. "Look, Damon, I can explain," he whispered, tugging on his arm. Freeing it, he sat up. "This isn't what it looks like."

"Who are you kidding, Justin? I can see very well what's going on. I'm just glad I convinced Elise to stay with Maria Teresa while I came looking for you."

"Elise is in Villa Vicencias?"

"Yes. We flew in yesterday."

He glanced at Melanie. "Oh, boy."

"That's one way of putting it. I suppose you're prepared to marry her?" he asked conversationally.

He stood up and picked up his folded jeans. "Of course I am. I love her."

Damon's smile lit up his face, and he relaxed for the first time since he walked into the room. He reached for Justin's hand as soon as he stepped into his jeans. "Welcome to the family. I couldn't be happier."

"Whoa, wait a minute. You still don't understand. Melanie doesn't want to marry me."

"She what?"

"Shh. Try not to wake her up. She's had a pretty rough time and needs her sleep. Come on downstairs and we'll have some coffee. I'll explain everything—if I can."

A few minutes later the two men left the room, quietly closing the door behind them.

When Melanie awoke she was surprised to find Justin gone. She vaguely remembered his returning last night. She'd heard the shower running but had been too sleepy to try to talk to him.

She sat up and stretched, grateful to be feeling better this morning. She would be seeing Maria Teresa by the end of the day. She would call her mother, and Elise and Damon, maybe even talk to Eric and Brenda. It was time to get back to the real world and quit living her fantasies.

After a quick shower she got dressed and hurried downstairs. No doubt Justin had gone down early for coffee.

She spotted him across the room, sharing a table with another man. The first thing she noticed was that they were speaking English. The second thing she noticed was that she knew the man with him.

"Damon!"

Damon stood up and turned around. "Hello, baby sister."

She flew into his arms. "Oh, Damon! It's great to see you. How did you get here? Where's Elise? How did you know where to find us?"

He started laughing. "Whoa, wait a minute. I can't answer everything at once. Here." He pulled a chair out for her, so that she sat on the third side of the table between him and Justin. He motioned the waiter for more coffee.

Melanie took the opportunity to look at Justin, but he refused to meet her eyes. She wondered how long Damon had been there and what Justin had told him.

Hopefully he remembered the story she had suggested.

After Damon was reseated he explained that Elise was with Maria Teresa. That he had left a rented car and driver on the other side of the river and that as soon as they had eaten and packed, there was a boat waiting to escort them across the river and to the car. They should be in Villa Vicencias by early afternoon.

"You're looking well and rested, Melanie. Did you get enough adventuring for your taste?" Damon's gray eyes danced, and Melanie wondered once again how much Justin had told him.

She smiled. "Actually it wasn't so bad, Damon. But transportation was a little hard to come by. I would have called if I could have, but there were no phones."

"Yes, that's what Justin explained."

"Oh? Well, then, you know what it's been like."

"Yes, I believe I do," he commented, leaning back so the waiter could place their breakfasts on the table.

While they ate the two men chatted as though they were sitting in their office. Damon caught Justin up on the negotiations. From what Melanie could gather, everything had functioned well while she and Justin were in Colombia. The men were laughing over how easily the deal went through when it looked as though Justin had lost interest.

If only Justin would look at her. Oh, he was polite enough, passing her things, asking if she needed anything, treating her as though she were Eric or Brenda sitting there with them.

She couldn't think of any way she could get him alone long enough to caution him about what to tell the family. There was no reason for anyone to know how they had spent their nights!

Now that their ordeal was behind them, Melanie could look back and treasure the time they had together.

"Are you ready to go?" Damon asked, and Melanie realized that Justin hadn't said anything to her since she had joined them, other than to see that she had everything she needed to eat.

"I need to go pack our things," she said, then stopped. Did Damon know they shared a room? Once again she darted a look at Justin, but he had asked Damon something else about the business. Damon didn't seem to notice her slip about packing "our" things. "I'll be right down," she added, and feeling as though she was escaping, she left the two men.

"So she doesn't want to marry you," Damon commented after she left.

"No."

"Did she give a reason why?"

"The more I thought about it, the more I realized she didn't have to. Her reasons were obvious."

"Not to me. What would you say they are?"

"She's too young for me. She has her own business, her own life. I'm too set in my ways."

"Is that what she said?"

"No."

"Then why don't you tell me what she said."

"What difference does it make?" Damon continued to watch him with a narrowed gaze that Justin recognized. He shrugged. "All right. She said she wasn't going to marry me because she knew I didn't want to be married."

"And how did she reach that conclusion?"

"Because I'm not already married."

"Of course she has a point there. Why aren't you married?"

"Because you keep me too damned busy to have a personal life," he said with a chuckle.

"And because—"

Justin added, more slowly, as though he were thinking out loud. "And because I was waiting for her to grow up."

Damon began to smile with quiet satisfaction. "I wondered if you were aware of that."

"What do you mean?"

"Oh, I've watched you over the years, listened to you, observed your behavior. From the time you first met her, you've treated other women as though you already had another commitment."

Justin was silent for a long while, thinking.

Eventually, Damon said, "I'll never forget the day you met her. She was staying with us in Chicago, remember?"

Justin nodded.

"You had been invited to dinner, and when she walked into the room you looked as though someone had clubbed you over the head. You seemed to have no idea what hit you."

"She was stunning," Justin agreed with a rueful smile.

"I know. I also saw your face when she explained that she was only nineteen years old. You were thirty or so by then, weren't you?"

"Yeah, as a matter of fact. I had recently turned thirty-one and felt like some cradle-robbing lecher because of the thoughts I was having about her."

Damon grinned. "I used to enjoy bringing her name into the conversation, just to watch you squirm."

Justin glanced up from his cup of coffee in surprise.

"I particularly enjoyed your reaction to Philip, the man who has so ardently pursued her for years," Damon added, obviously enjoying the scowl forming on Justin's face.

"Why, you no-good son-of-a—"

"Why, Justin. I'm surprised at you. And after all the things I've done for you," Damon said with a grin.

"You knew how I felt, and you put me through all that deliberately?"

"Well, actually, I was waiting to see when you intended to do something about the situation."

"I never intended to do anything about it."

"So I eventually realized."

Justin glanced at Damon with sudden suspicion. "Did you have anything to do with Melanie's deciding to come to Colombia?"

"Nothing at all. I haven't had anything to do with any of this. I've just observed. Oh, except for calling to let you know Melanie was missing."

"I'm glad you did."

"So am I. Regardless of your personal feelings, I still feel you were the best man for the job. Plus I figured that if you were forced to be around her for any length of time you would have to come to terms with your feelings." He leaned back in his chair. "Of course I don't know what Elise is going to think about your seducing her baby sister."

"My God, Damon! Do you intend to tell her?"

"Who, me? Why should I do that?"

Justin came to his feet and glared at his best friend as well as his employer. "It's nobody's business what went on between the two of us. Nobody's."

"I agree," Damon pointed out, as he stood up as well. "Are you ready to go?"

"Let me go check on Melanie."

Damon grinned. "Take your time. We've got all day. Elise can stand the suspense for a few more hours, I'm sure."

Justin tapped on the door and waited. When Melanie opened the door she was surprised to see him standing there. "Come in. I'm not used to your knocking. Don't you have your key?"

"Well, I, uh, thought I'd give you some privacy, if you needed it."

She grinned. "That's very sweet of you, Justin." She picked up his backpack. "I managed to get everything in there, although I'm not as good at packing as you are."

He took it from her and turned to the door.

"Justin?"

He glanced over his shoulder. "Yes?"

"What did you tell Damon about us?"

"What is there to tell?"

"I mean, did you tell him that we pretended to be married?"

"As a matter of fact, I did. I told him I didn't intend to let you out of my sight and that was the only way I could manage to stay with you."

"Oh." She thought about his explanation for a few minutes. "Do you think he'll tell Elise?"

"Your guess is as good as mine. At this point I have no idea what to expect from Damon. He revels in being mysterious and unpredictable."

How well she knew that. Although she loved her brother-in-law dearly, Melanie was the first person to admit that she had never understood him. She supposed it was enough that Elise did.

"Are you ready to go?" Justin asked, looking around the room once more.

"Yes, I'm ready." But she thought that might not be the exact truth. She wasn't at all sure she was ready to see Elise quite so soon after her week with Justin.

Eight

The car carrying Damon, Justin and Melanie no sooner pulled up in front of the large stucco home that belonged to Maria Teresa's family than the massive front door flew open. Maria Teresa and Elise rushed out. Melanie and Justin rode in the back seat while Damon sat in front with the driver, so it was an easy matter for Melanie to push the door open before they had come to a complete stop and throw her arms around both women. The three of them held each other and laughed, tears streaming down their faces.

Justin crawled out of the back seat behind her, glad to be through with riding for a while. The rough road and the detours made necessary because of downed trees had doubled their traveling time. Damon hadn't bothered to mention that he had started looking for them the evening before, within hours after he and Elise had landed. So he had been up all night. The grin on Damon's face made it clear he didn't regret the lost sleep.

"That's the first time Elise has laughed since we got word that Melanie was missing," he said quietly to Justin, who stood by his side. "I would have carried both of you on my back to her to see that expression on her face once again."

For the first time in his life, Justin could relate to the emotions Damon felt. He wondered why it had taken him so long to identify his feelings for Melanie. He almost wished he hadn't recognized them. Having her in his arms was going to be hard to forget.

Maria Teresa broke away from the other two and spoke to Justin. "You must be Justin Drake. I've heard so much about you. I'm glad we are meeting at last."

Maria Teresa was Melanie's opposite. She was tiny, with short, black curls that framed her elfin face. Her black eyes sparkled as she glanced back at Elise, then returned her gaze to Justin. "Thank you so much for bringing her safely to me."

"You're quite welcome."

"Please, everyone, let's go inside," Maria Teresa said. "You all must be tired. Dinner will be ready in an hour, then you must rest." They followed her into the house. A giant patio formed the center of the home, and each room on the first floor opened out onto it. A balcony ran around the second floor with its own flight of steps leading to the patio.

"What a beautiful home you have, Maria Teresa," Melanie enthused. "No wonder you used to get so homesick."

"Yes. I love it here. I hope you will, too."

She led them up the wide staircase and down a long hallway, pointing out each of their rooms.

"I, for one, am going to shower and get cleaned up," Damon announced. "I'll see all of you at dinner." He and Elise disappeared behind one of the bedroom doors.

"That sounds like a workable plan to me," Justin added. "I'll see you two later." He stepped into the room assigned to him and closed the door.

"Your room is next to mine," Maria Teresa explained. "I'm sure you are just as tired, aren't you?"

"Well, I'm tired, but I still want to talk. Can you stay while I soak in the tub? I want to hear all of your news."

"And I want to hear all of *your* news. We have all been so worried about you. You must tell me everything that happened." She followed Melanie into the bathroom and dumped bath oil into the water for her, found her a towel, then perched herself on the vanity stool. "And your Justin is even more handsome than you once told me."

"He isn't *my* Justin, you know. He came looking for me because Damon called and asked him to."

"Oh, I see. So he is not interested in you at all romantically."

"Of course not."

Maria Teresa's peal of laughter echoed around the small room. "Oh, Melanie. You are absolutely price-less. Who do you think you're talking to, anyway? I spent four years with you, and I can read you like a book. And you can't tell me the tension between the two of you is all one-sided. I refuse to believe that."

Melanie wrapped her braid around her head and secured it with some hairpins Maria Teresa handed her.

"Oh, Terri," she hadn't used that nickname in years, "I love him so much."

"Yes, I know. And the feeling is obviously mutual."

"So he says."

"But that's wonderful, Melanie. Now all he has to do is propose to you."

"He already has," she said gloomily.

"He has proposed, and you aren't happy about it? I don't understand."

"I turned him down."

"Obviously your recent ordeal has unhinged your mind." She watched as Melanie carefully crawled into the tub, sliding down until her chin touched the water. "I know it has been bad for you, my friend, but in a few days you will be able to adjust, then you can explain to him how you feel."

"I have no intention of doing that."

"Why not?"

"The only reason he offered to marry me is be-cause he made love to me."

"Oh, Melanie. I'm sure that isn't so. He isn't the type of person to take advantage of a situation."

"I didn't say he did. It was what we both wanted."

"So now you will marry and raise many children and be happy. What is wrong with that?"

"Think about it for a minute, Terri. Justin is thirty-seven years old. He has never been married. Why would he suddenly propose marriage now?"

Maria Teresa stared at her friend for a moment. "Because he loves you, of course."

"Because he knows that Damon would kill him if he didn't. Remember, I'm family. Also remember, my family has hovered over me since I was in the cradle. They would never allow anyone to hurt me. Justin knows that as well as I do."

"So marry him, anyway. You love him, don't you?"

"Of course I love him. I love him too much to see him unhappy. And he would be terribly unhappy if he got married, don't you see that?"

"Maybe not. Maybe he's ready to settle down. Maybe he wants to settle down with you."

"And maybe horses have wings and pigs can fly."

"Do you mean to tell me that you are going to give up the chance to marry Justin Drake because you're afraid he will be unhappy?"

Melanie nodded.

"That has to be the dumbest reason I ever heard. It will be up to you to see that he is not unhappy. And of course you can do that. Show him just how happy you can be."

"Do you think I can?"

"I know you can. I've never seen you give up on anything so easily before."

"That's because I've never wanted anything so much in my life before. And I'm afraid."

Maria Teresa laughed. "Don't be. I have a strong belief that he is on your side and wants the marriage to work as much as you do."

Melanie smiled dreamily. "Wouldn't that be nice?"

"More than nice. It would be marvelous. And just what you deserve." She stood up. "Look, I'm going to see how dinner preparations are progressing. Do you have something gorgeous to wear to dinner tonight?"

"Unfortunately, no. Most of my belongings were abandoned along the way."

"Let me check with Elise. Maybe she has something you can borrow."

Melanie smiled. "All right, matchmaker. I'll leave it to you."

During dinner there was a great deal of animated conversation. Whenever Justin was asked about anything regarding their experiences, he would neatly sidestep the question by bringing Melanie into it, thereby leaving her to say as much or as little as she wished.

"Actually, it wasn't bad at all," she explained. "We ran into problems with transportation after the mud slide. I was waiting for my guide to find me a way south when Justin found me." Neither of them mentioned her illness. "Later Justin ran into an old friend of his who let us borrow his Jeep." Justin took a quick sip of wine on that one. Melanie had missed her calling. She should have been a creative writer.

"We got as far as we could until we found the bridge out. That's when Damon found us." She smiled, picking up her glass and sipping from it.

"And here I was imagining all sorts of horrible things," Elise said with a soft laugh. "I feel a little silly now."

"I've always said you worried too much about me," Melanie chided gently. "I was never in any danger at all."

Unfortunately Justin had just taken another sip of wine and that outrageous lie caused him to choke. She stared him down while Damon thumped him on the back with a solicitous look on his face.

"But what about the earthquake? Weren't you somewhere near it?" Maria Teresa asked.

"The earthquake?" For a moment Melanie was at a loss for words. The earthquake represented such a special moment in her life she found herself embarrassed whenever it was mentioned.

She looked to Justin for assistance, but he was suddenly very busy with the food on his plate.

"Actually, we, uh, weren't all that close to the heavily damaged area." She waited to see if lightning would strike her. When nothing happened she let out a quick sigh and went on. "Of course we saw a lot of the area damaged as we traveled south. But we were very fortunate."

"Indeed you were," Damon added quietly.

Her eyes met his, and she could feel the heat of a blush in her cheeks. "I never did thank you for sending Justin to look for me."

"That's what family is for, little one. We aren't here to make your life so restrictive you can't enjoy it, but if we can protect you from harm, we want to...because we love you." His casual glance fell on Justin, then he turned to Elise with a smile. "Have you told Melanie about Brenda's latest exploration into the world of beauty, darling?"

The conversation effectively turned away from the events of the past few days and became centered on the antics of the children.

Melanie decided that she needn't have bothered to borrow a dress from Elise. Justin seemed to be totally unaware of her. The dress had matched the color of her eyes, the same shade of Elise's, and fit her very well. As soon as Elise had discovered that Melanie's clothes had not made it to Villa Vicencias, she had generously gone through what she had brought and divided it equally between them, letting Melanie choose what she wished to wear.

No one could have a more loving, a more generous sister than Elise, and Melanie felt humbled that she had someone who cared so much for her. Only now could she fully appreciate what the family must have gone through, waiting for some word that she was all right. She would have been the same way if Damon and Elise had suddenly dropped out of sight.

Melanie glanced over at Justin. He looked marvelous. Damon had obviously loaned him a change of clothing, as well, because she knew he had not brought a suit with him. The dark color enhanced his blond looks. He constantly amazed her. He appeared comfortable in a suit in a formal setting or in jeans and khakis in a jungle.

Justin Drake fit in wherever he was—quietly, without fanfare.

After coffee in the immense room that bordered the exquisite patio, Damon stretched and said, "If you will excuse me. It isn't the company, believe me. It's just that I'm getting too old to miss much sleep without it catching up with me."

His smile at Elise made it clear that he wasn't too concerned over his advancing age, and her answering grin reflected his lack of concern.

Melanie stood up. "I think I'll go up, as well." She looked around the room. "I'll see all of you in the morning."

Justin spoke up. "I'll probably be gone before you wake up, Melanie. I'm flying out at seven."

She stared at him in bewilderment. "You're leaving tomorrow?"

"Yes. I have quite a backlog of work to catch up on."

She tried to swallow the lump in her throat. "Of course. Well, then. I guess I'd better say my goodbyes now."

Damon and Elise had disappeared from the room, and when she looked around, Maria Teresa had mysteriously vanished, as well.

"I'll never forget what you did for me, you know," she said, walking over to where he stood looking out at the patio.

He continued to stare at the colorful profusion of plants. "I'm glad I could help. Of course we both know you could have managed just as well on your own. I appreciate the fact you didn't point that out to everyone."

"You know, Justin, I've learned a great deal from this experience, not least of which is that I don't need to prove my independence to people."

"That's true. You can take care of yourself and it shows. I don't imagine the family will hover quite so closely from now on."

"How about you? Do you intend to do any hovering?"

He glanced down at her for a moment, watching how the moonlight fell across her face, highlighting the soft sheen of her cheeks and forehead.

"No. I was never very good at that."

"You took to it like a pro, though. You kept Victor away from me."

"I suppose."

"What do you think happened to Victor? Do you think he got out all right?"

Remembering what he had seen in the rubble, he shrugged. "I'm sure Victor got what he deserved."

"I doubt that. He was a loathsome creature. I just hope we never run into him again."

"There's no reason to think we will."

"Well, I guess I'll go on to bed." She waited but he didn't say anything. "Aren't you going to kiss me goodbye?"

He leaned against the doorframe and faced her for the first time since they had been alone.

"I don't think that would be a good idea."

"Oh." So that was that. "Well. Thanks again," she said in a bright tone that sounded a little forced. "I'm sure I'll be seeing you again sometime—the next time you're in the States." She attempted a laugh that didn't quite work. "Who knows, I may visit you in Buenos Aires sometime."

"Good night, Melanie," he said in a firm voice, and she flinched.

Full of dejection, Melanie turned away and went upstairs.

When she woke up the next morning, he was gone.

Maria Teresa convinced Damon and Elise to stay for the week, so for the next several days the four of them toured the countryside. Melanie found many items that she knew would sell well in her shop, but her heart wasn't really into trying to add new lines of merchandise.

She couldn't get her mind off of Justin. How many nights had she lain awake because he wasn't there beside her? How could she have grown so used to sleeping with someone in such a short time?

Maria Teresa knew what was bothering her and tried to keep her too busy to think. Elise was another matter.

"I've never seen you like this, Melanie. You usually have more sparkle and zip than three people. Do you think you caught some sort of a bug in the jungle?"

"No. I'm just not sleeping well."

"Why not? Are you having nightmares or something?"

"Not really. I just wake up at every noise. I'll be all right in a few days, I'm sure," she said, then changed the subject.

Justin had been gone almost a week when he called Damon. "The papers are ready for your signature, boss. Where should I send them?"

"Why don't you fly them to me?" The company plane that had brought Damon and Elise to Colombia had flown Justin to Buenos Aires.

"I could, I suppose. But I'd rather not."

"I never thought of you as a coward, Justin."

"I don't consider myself a coward, either. I just don't see the point in needlessly inflicting pain on myself."

"She's miserable without you."

"Of course she is."

"You've given her time to think, which she needed. I believe the time is right for you to ask her again. I have a strong hunch you won't get a no this time."

Justin felt the heavy throb of his heart laboring in his chest. The thought of putting himself in the position of being turned down again terrified him. Perhaps he was more of a coward than he realized. To accept the fact that she didn't want him was easier on him than to live with the hope that she might, only to have that hope destroyed if she said no once more.

Feeling as though he was agreeing to face a firing squad, he said, "Whatever you say, boss. I'll see you sometime tomorrow."

He heard Damon laugh.

Justin suddenly remembered the months that Damon had waited to hear from Elise, and for the first time began to understand the pain caused by uncertainty when you really loved someone.

Was it possible Damon was right and that Melanie missed him?

He'd lost track of the nights he had lain awake, thinking about her: picturing her with the children in the square, putting lipstick on them; seeing her lying in bed, looking up at him with her eyes shining, her lips waiting for his possession; finding her holding little Miguel on her lap, soothing his fears; working alongside the doctor in the little hospital.

So he'd go back to see her. He might as well find out how he was going to adjust to the sight of her. As long as he worked with Damon, there would always be a chance that they would unexpectedly run in to each other.

Justin picked up the phone to alert the pilot that they were flying back to Villa Vicencias the next morning.

Nine

The women had spent the day shopping, and Elise swore she had bought out more than one little shop.

"I've never had so much fun," she said as they pulled into the driveway. "I feel guilty for barging in on your time together, but I've thoroughly enjoyed visiting with both of you."

Maria Teresa stopped in front of the main door. "Do you want out here, or do you want to go with me to the garage?"

"Oh, we'll go with you," Melanie said. "And as for you, Elise, I don't feel you've barged in on our visit at all, do you, Terri?"

"Of course not. The more the merrier." She glanced into the rearview mirror at Melanie in the back seat.

"As a matter of fact, she'd been a heck of a lot more fun this week than you have!"

Elise laughed. "She just doesn't want to admit that her trek through the jungle was too much for her."

"Yep, you found me out, all right. All that adventure and excitement was more than I could handle. Just give me the simple life." Melanie waved her hand at the other three vehicles parked in the long garage, then to the pile of packages the women had managed to accumulate during the day. They all three looked at one another and burst out laughing.

They were still laughing when they came into the hallway, trying to balance packages so they didn't have to make another trip to the car.

"I'm glad to see that you're all concerned with boosting the national economic level. Did you leave anything in the stores?" Damon stood outside the study, where he had been working while they were gone, and watched as they came to a laughing stop in front of him.

Elise kissed him. "Oh, we left a few odds and ends. We didn't want to appear greedy." A movement behind Damon caught her eye, and she looked past him. "Why, Justin, I didn't know you were coming. When did you get in?"

Melanie felt the packages slipping out of her hands, but she could do nothing about that. At the mention of his name her arms went numb. "Justin?" She stood there in the hallway, her packages scattered around her feet, and stared at him.

"Hi, Melanie," he said with commendable composure. "Looks like you could use some help." He bent over and gathered up her packages. "Here, I'll take these upstairs for you." He winked at Damon, a gesture no one else saw, and started up the stairs.

Maria Teresa said, "I don't know about you two, but I'm ready for some coffee."

"Me, too," Elise agreed. "Let me take these upstairs, find some more comfortable shoes, and I'll join you."

Damon nodded his agreement and went back to his work, stacking it neatly. Justin had done an excellent job of negotiation on the joint venture, and Damon had just offered him a partnership in Trent Enterprises.

Obviously surprised at the offer, Justin had accepted and seemed genuinely pleased. However, at the sound of the women's laughter Damon had totally lost Justin's attention. So much for the allure of big business.

Melanie opened the door for Justin and ushered him in. "Just toss them in that chair. I'll have to refold and pack them later."

Justin set the packages down, then turned around and looked at Melanie. It seemed more like months than days since he had last seen her, She appeared more rested, and there was a glow in her eyes he hadn't seen for a while. He hoped it was there for him.

He rested his hands on his hips. "Where's my tip?"

She looked startled. "Your tip?"

"I should get a kiss of gratitude, at least."

Melanie began to tremble. This was the teasing Justin that she remembered, not the cold, aloof man who had left days before. How could she resist him?

"I didn't think you wanted my kisses," she said, walking to him hesitantly.

"I never said I didn't want them. Just that they weren't a very good idea."

"Oh."

"But the more time I've had to think about them, the better the idea seems."

She paused in front of him, and he reached out for her. Her arms surged around his neck.

"I've missed you so much," he managed to say before his lips found her extremely kissable mouth.

She gave her reply without words, but he got her message. They stood locked together, his mouth reexploring hers, while Justin reacquainted himself with the scent, taste and feel of her.

"Coffee's ready," Elise's voice reached them as she passed down the hallway.

Justin reluctantly let go of her.

"Would you like some coffee?" Melanie's voice sounded husky.

"I'm sure it would be safer than our continuing to stay in this room alone together," Justin admitted with a slight smile.

He took her hand and led her out of the room.

By the time they reached the downstairs area, his hand rested lightly on her back and when Elise glanced up, she saw nothing unusual about Justin escorting Melanie into the room. They had probably become good friends since they had shared so much time together.

Melanie was ready to scream with frustration by the end of the evening. Everyone seemed to be enjoying themselves, of course, and Justin appeared more relaxed than he had been for some time. His gaze kept meeting Melanie's with a message that wasn't all that hidden, but there wasn't much she could do about it.

They never had a private moment. Damon sat watching everyone as though amused about something. Elise was bubbling with the news that she had talked with the children earlier in the evening, saying that although they missed her they were having the time of their lives with their grandmother on the farm.

A friend of Maria Teresa's had dropped by to visit. They had met him earlier in the week, all but Justin, and it was plain to him that Ric was totally enamored. *It takes one to know one,* he thought with a rueful smile. No doubt Ric was as frustrated at the lack of privacy as he was.

Justin considered asking Melanie to go out to the patio with him, but that was too obvious. She seemed sincerely pleased to see him, but that didn't mean she had changed her mind about marrying him.

He finally gave up and went to bed when everyone else did, sometime shortly after midnight.

There was no way he could sleep. After tossing and turning for almost an hour, Justin decided to enjoy the quiet night by sitting outside on the patio. He put on his jeans and a shirt, but didn't bother with the buttons. After quietly closing the door onto the balcony behind him, he silently walked around to the stairway that led to the beautifully laid out garden.

If Melanie had been asleep, she would not have heard the slight sound of a door closing. Obviously someone else was having trouble sleeping. She had tried everything. A warm bath, a boring book, her mathematical tables. But somehow all she could think about was that Justin was right next door to her.

She flung back the covers and grabbed her robe, one of her new purchases. It was as sheer as the gown she wore. She recognized that she bought the matched set with Justin in mind. She opened the door and tiptoed across the balcony to the railing.

Although the moon wasn't out, there was enough light from the stars for her to see that someone was down there. A glint of light caught and reflected the tawny color of Justin's hair and she grinned.

So he couldn't sleep, either. Without putting on her shoes, Melanie followed the same route Justin had used earlier.

He heard a sound near the stairs and turned around. Since his eyes had grown used to the dark, he immediately recognized her and the fact that she had very little on. Actually, there was some sort of gauzy material completely covering her, but it did nothing to conceal her womanly curves.

"You're going to catch cold out here," he pointed out in a low voice when she joined him.

She ran her hand slowly up his bare chest. "The same thing could be said for you." She felt his muscles contract at her touch and she smiled.

"When are you planning to go back to the States?" he asked, trying to keep his mind off the fact that her touch had caused his body to immediately respond to her.

"I haven't decided. I think Damon and Elise are leaving in a few days. She's anxious to get back home to her family." She lifted her head so that she could look up into the sky. "As for me, I don't know. I may never go home."

"What's that supposed to mean?"

"Maria Teresa and I have been talking about opening a business together down here. She's trying to give me a crash course in the language, and I'm teaching her the ins and outs of wholesale purchasing for retail selling."

"I figured you'd be ready to run home to mother after what we went through."

She laughed and shook her head. "No. What I learned was that I want more from life than my little shop has to offer. I may sell it or lease it. I haven't decided yet."

"What about marriage?"

"What about it?"

"Don't you want to marry someday?"

"You bet. But only the man I love."

"Oh."

"The crazy thing is that when he asked me to marry him, I didn't believe he really meant it, so like a fool I turned him down." Her other hand had come to rest against his chest. His skin felt hot, and she could feel the thudding of his heart against the palm of her hand.

"Do you have any idea what you are doing to me?" he managed to ask hoarsely.

"Probably the same thing you're doing to me," she responded candidly.

His hands came down at her waist, and he realized she had nothing on underneath the robe and gown she wore. "Don't play games with me, Melanie."

Her hands crept up around his neck, and she leaned her body against him. "I'm so glad you came back, Justin. I've never been so lonely in my life."

"It was probably a reaction due to all you've been through recently."

"That's one way of putting it. I certainly had a reaction to your lovemaking. It's become very addictive." She kissed him lightly on the chin.

"God! Melanie, you are driving me crazy," he muttered. Blindly he lowered his head and found her mouth with his. He crushed her to him while his mouth devoured hers with an intense need that cut through any pretense that might have existed between them.

She reveled in his possession. When he pulled away slightly, she smiled up at him trustingly. He began to place tiny kisses across her face, on her eyelids, in front of her ear and along her jawline until he could no longer resist her mouth once again.

She sighed contentedly. As long as she was in Justin's arms, everything was fine in her world.

His hands had not been still. They found the rounded fullness of her breasts, and he lowered his head to kiss each one. His hand glided down her side to her thigh, then slowly moved between them. Her knees gave way and he quickly braced her against him, his legs spread so that she rested on him.

The feel of his hard body giving her nonverbal proof of his arousal increased the flame that had begun to flicker inside of her.

"Melanie, I want you so much," he whispered.

"I want you, too."

"But I don't want you just for tonight. It would destroy me to love you, then walk away. I did it once. I can't do it again."

"You don't have to walk away from me, Justin. Not ever. I'll go wherever you want me to go."

He raised his head and looked at her, trying to read her expression. "Does that mean you'll marry me?"

"Yes."

"You mean that?"

"Yes."

"Even if I'm too old for you, too set in my ways—"

"Is this a proposal or a confession?" she asked with interest.

"You didn't want to marry me when I asked earlier."

"I did so. But not if you were only asking to be polite."

"Me? Polite? You must have me confused with someone else."

"I decided that even if you never thought about getting married before I'll make you so happy you won't have a chance to regret it."

He nuzzled underneath her chin. "I will never regret marrying you."

I hope not, she prayed. His hands were exploring her with a possessiveness that she found highly inflammatory. She shivered as he undid the tie at her waist.

"You're cold. I told you you would be."

"Are you going to be one of those husbands who always points out when he's right?"

"I'll try to control those tendencies."

"Good."

He picked her up and started up the staircase. "We'd better continue this discussion in the morning."

"It is morning."

"After daylight."

"Everyone else is asleep. Why don't you spend the rest of the night with me? I can't seem to sleep without you."

He paused at her doorway. She had left the door slightly ajar, and he pushed it farther open with his elbow. "I have the same problem. The only trouble is that if I stay in here with you, we probably won't get any sleep, either."

He slowly lowered her to the bed. She took the opportunity to slip off her robe. The nightlight from the bathroom gave enough light for Justin to see that her gown was transparent.

She moved over on the bed, and her gown crept up around her thighs. "Well, let's be logical about this.

Would you rather not sleep alone or not sleep together?''

He grinned. "I guess I never looked at it quite in those terms before."

"You can slip out early in the morning, can't you?"

"I'm sure I can. The question is, will I?"

"I'll remind you."

"You do that."

By the time he had finished speaking, Justin had whisked the gown over her head and tossed it on the floor. His shirt and jeans soon followed.

For the next several hours Justin taught Melanie how much he loved her. He touched and caressed her, he teased and controlled her, he tantalized and completed her, making her a part of him. It was almost dawn when they fell asleep exhausted, wrapped in each other's arms. Justin stirred briefly, enough to find the covers and draw them around both of them—to ward off the chill to their overheated bodies.

Neither of them heard the sounds of the house stirring the next morning, nor the gentle tap on Melanie's door. The first they realized that Justin had forgotten to return to his room was when they heard Elise say, "Melanie, Damon has suggested that—oh, my God."

Melanie raised her tousled head from Justin's shoulder and peered at her sister who stood three steps or so inside the bedroom and looked as though she'd been turned to stone.

Elise turned away, blindly, and walked out of the room, closing the door quietly behind her.

"Oh, hell," Justin muttered disgustedly. "Now I've gone and blown everything."

Melanie sat up in bed. "You haven't done anything, Justin. Why do you keep trying to take the blame for something we've done together?"

"Because I'm older and should know better. I've had more experience and—"

"I don't want to hear about all your damned experience, Justin. And I'm rapidly becoming tired of hearing about your advanced years, Oh Aged One. Just for the record—"

Justin folded his arms behind his head and stared up at the ceiling. "Something tells me that our marriage isn't going to be one of those made-in-heaven affairs." He dropped his gaze and looked at her from the corner of his eye. "You aren't going to be one of those biddable wives, are you?"

Melanie stared at him in astonishment. "Is that what you want?"

He burst out laughing. "No, thank God, I don't. Otherwise I would never have fallen in love with you." He sat up and kissed her pouting mouth. "We've shocked enough people today. I'm going to my room, get cleaned up and try to find a way to apologize to my future sister-in-law for loving her baby sister not too wisely but all too well." He paused at the door to the balcony and looked back at her. "By the way, when are you going to marry me?"

"Noon?"

He nodded. "Maybe, just maybe, that will save me. We can only hope."

* * *

When Damon came out of the shower he found Elise sitting in a straight-backed chair, staring blankly out the window. She looked very pale and when he came closer, he saw that she was worrying a handkerchief between her trembling fingers.

"What's wrong, Elise? You look like you're going to faint."

Slowly she turned her head, her eyes wide, filled with unshed tears. "You think you know someone, that you've known them for years, and then you suddenly discover you don't know them at all."

Damon felt his heart stop beating for a couple of beats, then it began to race. "Darling. What is it? Is it something I've done?" He knelt beside her, taking her hands in his. They felt cold, and the trembling upset him as much as the coldness.

"I'll never forget when I first met him. I was so impressed with his quiet strength, his loyal support, his ability to care deeply about someone."

Damon felt like he'd been punched right over the heart. For a moment he couldn't get his breath. "Are you telling me that you've fallen in love with someone else?"

Her eyes focused on him—on his worried look, the anguish in his eyes—and the tears began to spill over. "Oh, Damon, I trusted him. I trusted him with your life, with mine, with our children. And I trusted him with Melanie. Oh, God!" Because he still held her hands she couldn't use them to cover her face, so she sat there, tears running down her cheeks.

Damon tried to breathe and discovered his lungs were still working. "Are you talking about Justin?" he asked, his heart attempting to function once again after the near-fatal shock it had received.

"Yes, I'm talking about Justin. Justin, who pretended to be our friend while all the time he was seducing my sister!"

Lights and bells began to go off inside Damon's head, and he pulled Elise out of the chair and walked her to the bed, where he coaxed her to lie down. "Why don't you tell me what has just happened to upset you so, love? I'm sure there's a perfectly reasonable explanation."

"Oh, I'm sure that's true. The only trouble is, I don't want to hear any explanations. I know what I saw!"

"And what was that?"

She gulped. Did she really want Damon to know? Wouldn't it break his heart to know his friend had betrayed him? She tried to get a grip on her emotions.

"Tell me," he said in his quiet voice that, nevertheless, carried a great deal of authority.

"I was just checking on Melanie to tell her you had suggested that the four of us..." Her voice trailed off. "That's right. You had already decided that we would form two couples today since Maria Teresa was busy all day." She sat up. "Damon, did you know anything about this?"

"Just tell me what you saw, Elise."

"I found Justin in bed with Melanie."

"I see."

"You aren't shocked."

"Not particularly."

"Because you don't care what happens to my sister!"

"Elise, listen to me for a moment. Try to look at Melanie, not as your sister but as a grown woman. She is twenty-five years old. She is a mature, responsible adult who just happens to be your sister, okay?"

She nodded.

"All right. I doubt that I am breaking any confidences at this late date when I tell you that Justin has been in love with her for years."

"He has?"

"Definitely. But I don't think he realized it himself until he came rushing down here to rescue her."

"Oh."

"Things were a little rougher than Melanie was willing to share with you, but I'm getting a little tired of everybody in the family protecting everybody else's feelings. Especially at the risk of having Justin's motives misunderstood. Justin is an honorable man. All those things you said about him are true. When they were kidnapped by a cocaine smuggler—"

"Kidnapped!"

He ignored the interruption and went on. "Justin led the guy to believe he and Melanie were married so he could insist they not be separated."

Elise's eyes grew wide with astonishment while Damon continued. "So, for over a week Justin and Melanie lived together, ate together, slept together. He barely let her out of his sight."

He got up, walked over to the window and looked out. "Try to imagine what it would be like, say if you and I were thrown into that kind of dangerous situation, not sure if we were going to get out alive—" he heard her gasp but chose to ignore it "—and feeling the way we do about each other. Do you think we could live that close and not make love?"

"Well, of course not!"

He laughed at her indignation. "Neither could Justin and Melanie."

"Do you mean she loves him?"

He turned around and looked at her. "What do you think? Do you think your sister is the kind of woman who would go to bed with someone she didn't love and want to marry?"

The shocks were coming too thick and fast. "Marry?" she echoed faintly.

"That's what all of this is about. Justin asked Melanie to marry him, and he gave her some time to think about it." He hoped Justin and Melanie would forgive him for playing with the truth, but dammit, they had stuck him with pleading their case to his own wife! "He came back yesterday for his answer. Obviously he got the one he hoped for."

Elise sat there, dazed at the amount of information that had been poured over her. "I had no idea," she finally murmured. "Melanie never let on at all how she felt about him."

"I know. As far as she knows, neither one of us had any idea."

"But Justin had confided in you, hadn't he?"

Damon grinned. "Not exactly. Not until I found them sleeping together in a small village north of here."

"You mean you walked in on them like I did?"

"I think I'm going to buy them a lock for their bedroom door for a wedding gift. Can't think of a more practical one."

Elise's sense of humor began to reassert itself. "You mean you discovered them together and started playing the heavy-handed brother-in-law?" she asked, her eyes beginning to dance.

"Something like that," he admitted.

"Oh, I wish I had been there to see it."

"Do you? After the way you reacted this morning?"

"Well, it was such a shock."

"Tell me about it," he agreed, nodding. "I was ready to tear him apart, slowly and thoroughly."

"Oh, Damon." She shook her head, still chuckling. "I guess we owe Justin an apology."

"Like hell we do. The best thing we can do is to stay out of their business and let them decide how to live their lives. We sure as hell didn't listen to anyone else, did we?"

"No."

"Then it's time to let baby sister go, Elise. She's got Justin to look after her."

She nodded. "I feel like a complete idiot, walking in on them like that. How am I ever going to be able to face them again?"

Damon pulled her close to him and gave her a long, lingering kiss. "Oh, you'll think of something," he finally said. "I have complete faith in you."

Ten

Melanie brushed her hair, taking her time because she was thinking about Justin. Her mind seldom wandered far from him. He had really been upset when Elise had discovered them in bed together.

She stopped brushing and stared at her reflection in the mirror in surprise. He had been much more upset than she was.

How strange. For years Melanie had concerned herself with what her family thought, spent all kinds of energy resisting the pressures they brought to bear on her, and in fact, had wasted a considerable amount of time reacting to them, rather than living the life she wanted to live.

How interesting. Her repeated demands for independence, her need for excitement and adventure, had caused her to miss a vital message about herself. She could be whoever she wanted to be. She could act—not react. It didn't matter what they expected of her or wanted her to do or become. She could express herself, her identity, in any way she chose.

It had taken getting to know Justin to recognize that. He didn't go around demanding or enforcing respect. He knew his own worth and didn't need to remind anyone who he was. He just was.

She smiled. And he loved her; that was the greatest miracle of all. She glanced at the time. It was almost nine o'clock. She wondered if he really expected to marry her at noon. If so, she had better hurry.

Rapidly braiding her hair and wrapping it in a coil at the nape of her neck, Melanie tried to decide what to wear for a wedding. No. That was one decision she would wait to get advice on. What could be nicer—her sister and her best friend were here to help her plan a wedding.

She wondered if Damon would have his shotgun openly displayed. Poor Justin. No doubt he was already downstairs facing her irate relatives while she dreamed and dawdled upstairs. That was not fair of her at all.

Hurriedly she began to dress.

Justin came down the stairs and turned toward the dining room.

"We're eating out here this morning," Damon said from the patio. A breakfast table had been arranged with an umbrella for shade. Justin slowly turned his steps toward his friend.

"Actually I'm the only one down yet," Damon cheerfully admitted as he poured Justin a cup of coffee from a steaming carafe. "Maria Teresa has already left for her meetings today," he explained with uncharacteristic chattiness. He picked up his cup and sipped on the coffee. "Mmmmmmm. You can't beat the taste of Colombian coffee, that's for sure," he said blandly.

Justin knew his friend too well to go along with his urbane manner. "I know I was a stupid fool, so why don't you just come out and say so?"

Damon lifted his brow slightly. "I take it she said yes this time," he said with a slight smile.

Justin's color deepened slightly. He nodded.

"Good. When's the wedding to be?"

"Melanie suggested noon today."

Damon sprayed coffee all over his freshly pressed shirt, and Justin felt an odd sense of satisfaction at giving him just a little of what he was so good at dishing out—the unexpected.

"Noon...! Today?"

"That's what she said."

"What the hell's the big rush? I thought you told me she wasn't pregnant."

Justin glanced around the area in disgust. "I did and she isn't, but you don't need to broadcast the news, dammit."

Damon grinned. "Sorry. Then what's the big hurry?"

"It seems that Melanie and I have developed a bit of a problem as a result of our jungle adventure."

Damon frowned but before he could say anything, Justin continued.

"We got used to sleeping together and now can't sleep very well alone."

Damon gazed at the shadows beneath his friend's eyes. "You don't look as though you got all that much sleep last night."

"We intend to work on that."

"I just bet you do." Damon started laughing. He would pause, look at the expression on Justin's face and begin to laugh all over again.

He was still chuckling when Elise joined them. She smiled at the two men—her usual warm, serene smile, and for a moment Justin was convinced he had dreamed that she had walked into Melanie's room earlier that morning. "Good morning. I seem to have missed something funny. Care to share the joke?"

Justin sipped on his coffee and waited for Damon to begin raking him over the coals.

"I'm just amused to think that after all of this time our friend Justin here has decided to get married. I never thought I'd live to see it happen."

Elise watched while Damon poured her coffee, then she picked it up and daintily took a sip. "Mmm, I don't think I've ever tasted better coffee."

She couldn't understand why her perfectly innocent comment should send both men into more laughter. She sniffed the coffee carefully. Could they have spiked it with something?

"Good morning," Melanie sang out as she came swinging out of the house. "Isn't it a beautiful morning?"

Elise watched the two men carefully for signs of another attack of unexplained laughter. Apparently their sense of humor didn't run to beautiful mornings. "Yes," she finally agreed. "It certainly is. However, if you feel the need to comment on the coffee, be prepared to be met with howls of laughter."

Elise eyed both men sternly.

Melanie sank down in the remaining chair and stared around the table, bewildered. "What are you talking about?"

Elise shrugged. "I wish I knew. Frankly I'm afraid these two got into the liquor cabinet this morning."

"That isn't true," Damon protested. "We are being unjustly maligned." He straightened in his chair slightly, giving both Melanie and Justin the benefit of his devilishly attractive grin. "Actually we were talking about weddings and things. Like when, where— that sort of thing."

Justin had taken Melanie's hand when she sat down, and he felt her stiffen at Damon's words. Was she going to resent her family's interest in their wedding? He sincerely hoped not, because they were the closest thing to family he had. But he recognized that it was something she was going to have to work out.

Melanie grasped Justin's hand in a firmer grip and announced, "Justin and I are going to be married." There was a hint of defensiveness, but only a hint.

Elise smiled. "I couldn't be happier. I think you are perfect for each other."

Neither Justin nor Melanie expected that reaction from Elise, particularly not after what had happened earlier.

"Have you set a date yet?" she asked.

"Well, we, uh, thought we'd check with you two," Melanie began, "see what your plans are and everything, then—"

Damon spoke up. "How about noon today?"

"Today!" Elise echoed. "Oh, Damon, that would be impossible. Surely she'll want to shop for a dress and plan some sort of reception...." Her voice trailed off as she noticed the expression on Melanie's face. She was staring first at Damon, then at Justin, then back at Damon.

"You told him, didn't you," she said to Justin with some irritation.

"I told him I wanted to marry you as soon as possible."

"Sounds like a good plan to me," Damon explained. "Does anyone have any idea how you go about getting married in Colombia?"

Everyone looked at everyone else. Nobody knew.

"Maria Teresa would know," Melanie finally said. "We'll have to wait and ask her."

"Well, then," Damon pointed out in a reasonable tone of voice, "it doesn't look as though you two are going to be able to get married today after all. That's really too bad. Perhaps you'd better plan to take sleeping pills for the next few nights.''

"Damon!" Elise remembered quite well what Damon preferred to use for a sleeping pill.

Justin and Melanie couldn't understand Elise's reaction to Damon's remark, and they stared at her in bewilderment. Damon realized how Elise had interpreted it and he started laughing again, the looks on the faces of the three people sitting around him causing him to fight for his breath.

Damon Trent couldn't remember a day when he had laughed so hard. Nor could he remember a day when he was so happy for those he loved. He'd have to try to remember to tell Elise what the joke was later that night when they were alone.

"Happy first anniversary, darling," Justin whispered near Melanie's ear. She opened her eyes and saw that there was barely enough light in the room to see.

"Justin, it isn't even daylight yet."

"I didn't want to miss any of today, so I thought we'd get an early start." He slipped his hand under the covers and stroked her hip and thigh. "Are you really so sleepy?"

She moved her head on his shoulder, butting it lightly against his chin. "Well, you did keep me awake quite late last night, you know."

"I didn't hear you make a single complaint."

"Nope," she admitted. "Not a one."

"You don't want to waste today sleeping, do you?" he asked in an incredulous tone.

"Apparently not," she agreed. Melanie sat up in bed. She glanced over at the man who held her heart in the palm of his hand. Why had she fallen in love with a morning person? Surely there was some reason that had happened to her. She wished she understood what it was.

"I thought I'd take you out to breakfast, then after that we could go for a drive—"

"Today is Tuesday, Justin. Don't you intend to go into the office?"

"On my anniversary? Don't be silly."

"It's your anniversary, not a national holiday."

"I think I'll talk to Jorge about that. He knows everybody in the government. As a matter of fact, I think he's related to everybody in the government. Maybe we can get them to pass a law making today a—"

She held up her hand. "Forget it. Okay, so you're taking today off. Does Maria know that?"

"It's been marked on the calendar for weeks."

She stared at him closely. "You're really serious about this, aren't you?"

"You're damned right. This date will stick in my memory until I die. I never had so much trouble getting married in all of my life. I didn't think I'd live to see the day."

Melanie giggled. "It wasn't that bad!"

"Says you. You didn't care how long it took to cut through the red tape, fly your mother, niece and nephew down to Colombia, plan a reception—you were having too much fun shopping with your mother, sister and girlfriend.''

She sighed. ''I know. It was wonderful.''

''Right. Wonderful. You didn't even care how many cold showers I was forced to take while we waited.''

''Well,'' she pointed out reasonably, ''I could hardly have you sharing my room while we prepared for the wedding. If you think Elise had a bad reaction to the idea, can you imagine what Mother would have done?''

''I don't want to think.''

''Anyway, you got to plan the honeymoon.''

''What honeymoon?''

''*Our* honeymoon.''

''Melanie, we never had a honeymoon. I brought you directly back to Buenos Aires, kept you in bed for three days and then I had to get back to work.''

''I know. It was wonderful,'' she said with a sigh.

''Lady, you are easy to please.''

She grinned. ''I didn't find you too terribly hard to entertain, myself.''

He found that particular mischievous grin impossible to ignore and he reached for her. Just as she tumbled into his arms, he halted. ''No. I'm not going to do this.''

''Do what?''

''I am not going to spend my first anniversary of marriage making love to you.''

''Why not?''

"Because I want to take you out, show you off, take you dancing, see a show, go to the coast, do something really special to show you how much I love you."

"Justin?"

"Hmm?"

"Don't you think I know you love me every time you make love to me?"

"Well, it's a pretty fair indication of my feelings when I can't keep my hands off of you."

"So you have found perfectly wonderful ways to show me you love me."

"Does that mean you don't want to go out for breakfast? Go for a drive? Go to a show? Go dancing?"

"I just want to be with you, doing whatever makes you happy."

He nuzzled her neck. "This makes me happy." He reached down and kissed her on the breast. "This makes me happy." He found the ticklish spot just under her navel and kissed her, enjoying how she squirmed. "This makes me happy."

For a long while there was nothing but soft moans and whispers until finally Justin muttered. "Oh, what the hell. Maybe by our tenth anniversary we'll be able to make it out of bed in time for breakfast!"

Silhouette Desire
COMING NEXT MONTH

TOO HOT TO HANDLE—Elizabeth Lowell
Rancher Ethan Reeves quickly exposed his devilish nature to Tory. With his cold eyes and dark presence, she refused to ask him for anything—until she discovered he was really an angel in disguise.

LADY LIBERTY—Naomi Horton
Genevieve needed to protect her grandfather's name by destroying a forgery of the priceless Liberty stamp. But she ran into Griff in the process and found he was a thief—after her heart.

A FAIR BREEZE—Ann Hurley
Leah wasn't interested in involvement—especially in a nosy New England village. But Jonathon Wardwell, the local carpenter, had a plan—and she played a major role.

TO MEET AGAIN—Lass Small
He'd kissed her once, and Laura's marriage hadn't survived the molten memory. Time hadn't extinguished that golden passion, and when Tanner held her, she knew she couldn't leave him again.

BROOKE'S CHANCE—Robin Elliott
A friendly bet landed Brooke on the lap of a department store Santa, and Chance quickly assessed the beauty in his arms. Could she overcome her fears and accept his gift of love?

A WINTER WOMAN—Dixie Browning
Delle's bird-watching college cronies would stop at nothing to find her a man, but she hadn't expected Cyrus, a golden-crested *handimanus hunkus*, who succeeded in setting her soul on fire.

AVAILABLE NOW:

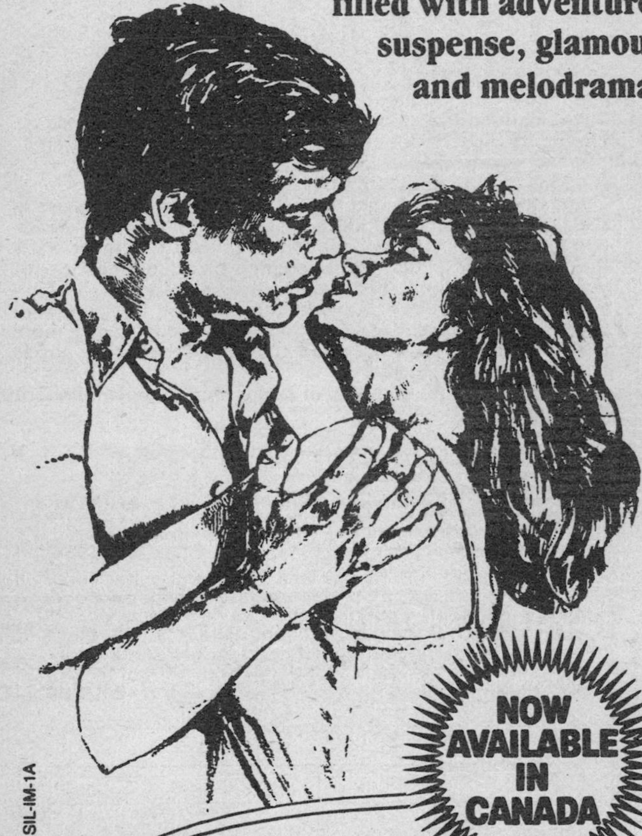